SARANORMAL

Giving Up
the Ghost

by Phoebe Rivers

SIMON SPOTLIGHT
New York London Toronto Sydney

SIMON SPOTLIGHT
An imprint of Simon & Schuster Children's Publishing Division
1230 Avenue of the Americas, New York, New York 10020
Copyright © 2013 by Simon & Schuster, Inc.
All rights reserved, including the right of reproduction in whole or in part in any form.
SIMON SPOTLIGHT and colophon are registered trademarks of Simon & Schuster, Inc.
Text by Sarah Albee
For information about special discounts for bulk purchases, please contact Simon & Schuster Special Sales at 1-866-506-1949 or business@simonandschuster.com.
Manufactured in the United States of America 0113 OFF
First Edition 10 9 8 7 6 5 4 3 2 1
ISBN 978-1-4424-6617-3 (pbk)
ISBN 978-1-4424-6616-6 (hc)
ISBN 978-1-4424-6618-0 (eBook)
Library of Congress Catalog Card Number 2012938943

Chapter 1

Snowflakes swirled around me as I clenched my arms against my middle and shrugged my shoulders, shivering in my thin T-shirt, blue jeans, and sneakers. The wind whipped my hair around my face, but I was too cold to reach up and tuck it behind my ears. My body shook. My teeth chattered. Why hadn't I worn a coat?

I worked my half-frozen fingers into my front pocket, searching for my Christmas list. But my pocket was empty. I scuffed my sneaker through the powdery snow in frustration and immediately regretted it. Snow quickly soaked through the thin canvas of my sneakers, sending fresh shivers up and down my spine.

Holiday shoppers bustled past me on the busy street, laden down with packages and looking warm and happy, bundled up in their parkas, wrapped in scarves, cozy in their knit hats. The shops along Beach Drive were brightly lit, twinkling with lights and decorated with Christmas stuff. Again I wondered why I was outside with no coat on.

Then I saw her.

The crowd seemed to part like curtains. She stood alone on the sidewalk, wrapped in a fancy-looking winter coat. Her head darted back and forth like a bird. She looked nervous. Wary. Suspicious. I'd never seen her before, yet I couldn't shake the feeling that she was somehow familiar to me.

She was a very strange-looking woman. Her eyes were the color of antifreeze. She had thin lips and a long, hooked nose. Her hair was snow white, but her smooth skin made me wonder if she was old enough to have white hair. She could be anywhere from thirty-five to sixty-five. Maybe she was one of those people, I thought, who have had such a sudden, nasty shock that their hair turns white overnight.

And then, as if someone had just turned up the volume on a radio, I heard her thoughts.

. . . can't take this . . . get away from the crowd . . . that way, that way . . .

Followed almost immediately by the thoughts of everyone else who was passing by.

. . . get that scarf for Uncle George? . . . Did I send a card to the Nelsons? . . . The flight gets in tomorrow morning . . .

They were all just snippets. Fragments.

I had been able to hear other people's thoughts for weeks now. Not always. And not everyone. But it was happening more and more. This was a new power. To add to the ones I already had.

I'd been able to see spirits—dead people—for as long as I could remember. Recently that power had intensified, and for a while now I'd been able to inter-act with the spirits, to talk with them. Since I'd arrived in Stellamar last summer, I had gradually come to accept these powers. Before moving here, back when I lived in California, I'd hated them. They made me feel different, and I just wanted to be normal. But with my great-grandmother's help, I was actually starting to look at them as the "gift" she insisted they were. Most of the time, anyway.

But this new power was different. I wasn't sure I liked being able to listen in on what people were thinking. Sometimes you heard things you wished you hadn't.

Now my head was pounding—the thoughts of multiple passersby crowded inside my head, bouncing around inside my brain and practically deafening me. It was like someone tuning a radio, from station to station, rapidly and on high volume. Or like being in a very crowded, noisy room with terrible acoustics.

Suddenly I realized that the strange woman could also hear people's thoughts, because she jumped when people passed by, as though their thoughts grew louder, the way they were doing in my own mind. And she looked as though she hated this scrambled, deafening noise as much as I did.

The woman hustled across the street, weaving her way between shoppers. She scurried under the huge sign that announced the Stellamar Boardwalk. Ignoring my instincts, which were telling me to run, not walk, as fast as I could away from the woman, I followed her. My feet seemed propelled by a will of their own.

As I emerged onto the windy, weather-beaten boardwalk, I saw her leaning on the railing and looking out at the slate-gray, choppy waters. Curling wisps of snow tumbled and danced between us. We were the only ones. No one else in their right mind would willingly stand there, bearing the full brunt of the icy December wind off the ocean.

The woman didn't notice me. She seemed way too absorbed in her own thoughts, staring out at the ocean. Now I could hear her thoughts clearly, because they were no longer mixed up with the thoughts of all the other people.

Must stop . . . Can't do this anymore . . . Why? Why did I not stop when I had the chance?

As I watched, a scrap of paper fluttered and swirled around the woman in an erratic figure eight on the whirling wind. It hovered gently in the air in front of her, like a butterfly about to alight on a flower. As if in a daze, she plucked the paper from the wind and stared at it.

I was at least ten steps away from her, but I could clearly see what it was. A copy of one of the flyers my best friend, Lily Randazzo, and I had made last fall. We'd made a bunch of them to help advertise my great-grandmother's business and hung them all over the boardwalk. LADY AZURA! PSYCHIC, HEALER, MYSTIC.

The woman stared at the paper. I heard her thoughts.

Lady Azura is still in business? Well then, I will go to her. I will make her help me.

She seemed to know my great-grandmother! Maybe I should approach her. Offer to help. But something stopped me. She seemed angry. Hostile. And what did she *want*? Suddenly I felt wary. Protective of Lady Azura.

My teeth began to chatter. From the cold or from my fear, I wasn't sure. But probably both.

She folded up the paper and shoved it into her coat pocket. I had just decided that the best thing to do would be to run the other way when she wheeled around and faced me. Bored a hole through me with those eerie green eyes.

I forgot all about how cold I was. My heart pounded in my ears. I felt as though that green, probing stare was hypnotizing me. Like it was drawing me toward her, and I could fall in and drown. She was so strange-looking. Not old, not young. Fierce. Determined-looking. I thought about running home to warn Lady Azura that this weird woman might be showing up.

She tilted her head back and laughed. "Weird woman?" she said in a mocking voice. "You want to warn Lady Azura that I might be showing up? That is an excellent idea. But there's nothing she can do. *Nothing!*"

She'd heard my thoughts. Read my mind.

"The damage has been done!" she said, pointing at me. "The energy has been released."

Now I was officially freaked out. I turned to run away. Fast. I ran. Tripped and fell.

And then I woke up.

I was in my darkened bedroom. I was all twisted up in my sheets. My hair was plastered to my forehead with sweat. My heart was thudding like a big bass drum.

I managed to kick away my covers. I sat up and looked at the clock. My mind was groggy. It felt like the middle of the night. But the clock read seven fifteen. Why was it so dark in my room? It was too dark to be past seven a.m. on a morning in March. For a moment I had the strangest thought, that there was a cloud in my room, hovering over my bed. I stared up into it and tried to make sense of how this was possible, wondering if I was still asleep.

After closing my eyes and opening them a few more times, I realized it wasn't dark in my room at all. It was a bright, sunny day. The window was open. I could smell the fresh sea breeze blowing off the ocean. I could hear birds twittering, and smell coffee brewing. The darkness in my room had been my imagination. It had to have been. It was a beautiful, sunny morning. Not a cloud in the sky, let alone one in my bedroom.

I swung my legs around and got out of bed.

That had been one weird dream.

Chapter 2

Yesterday's jeans were lying on the floor next to my bed. I tugged them on. They were nicely stretched out and comfy where my body had molded them the day before. I grabbed a T-shirt from the pile of clean laundry on my dresser and quickly surveyed my outfit in the mirror. Fabulous it wasn't, but it would do. I quickly ran a brush through my long blond hair and pulled it into a ponytail.

I wasn't all that concerned about fashion. A stark contrast to Lily, who always looked great. We were total opposites on a lot of things, but it somehow just worked for us. She was from a huge, bustling family. In the town of Stellamar, practically every person you met was a Randazzo or a close relative. I had just my dad and my great-grandmother. Lily was outgoing;

I was shy. She loved being the center of attention. The idea of being the center of attention gave me palpitations.

Having a best friend still felt new and strange. In a good way. I smiled a little. I loved saying the phrase "my best friend."

As my eyes scanned my bedroom, looking for my sneakers, I spotted my favorite picture of my mother, which I kept on the bedside table. In it, she was sitting on a big rock, her legs pulled up to her chin, and she was grinning at the photographer—my dad. She was so beautiful. My dad told me that people used to stare at her all the time because she was so pretty, and I believe it. She died giving birth to me.

My dad and I had come to live with Lady Azura, my great-grandmother, at the end of last summer. She and I had something in common: the power to see the spirits of the dead.

We'd moved from California to this seaside town in New Jersey and into this ramshackle Victorian house owned by my great-grandmother. My dad was slowly making repairs to the house, and it was looking better than when we had first arrived. And we were just a few blocks away from the beach, which was pretty cool. Dad and I lived on the top two floors, and Lady Azura lived downstairs, but we shared the big, roomy kitchen. Slowly the boundaries between her space and ours had blurred. Now it mostly just felt like a family living together.

In the large bay window near the front door of the house, Lady Azura had hung a gold-and-purple-lettered sign, advertising herself as a psychic, healer, and mystic. She met clients on the first floor, although over the fall and winter they hadn't been coming around very often. Maybe once or twice a week at most. Her business tended to pick up during the summer tourist season. On rainy days, when people weren't able to go to the beach, business could get downright busy, or so she'd told me.

As I headed down the stairs to breakfast, I glanced into the sitting room. I glimpsed one of the spirits who inhabited our house—the grumpy Mr. Broadhurst—pacing near the window. It felt weirdly comforting to see him there. I saw him most mornings, along with a handful of other spirits who shared the house with us: an older woman spirit, sitting in a chair on the porch, knitting; a younger woman in the upstairs pink bedroom, who often rocked in a rocking chair, crying, I had learned, about her son who had died a long, long time ago. There were others, too. I no longer got the nauseous feelings, the unpleasant tingling in my leg, when I felt the presence of the spirits in our house. I was used to them. They were part of my house.

As I entered the kitchen, I was surprised to see Lady Azura sitting at the kitchen table, gloomily stirring her tea and staring into space. She was not one to get up early. We rarely saw her up and around before eleven a.m. And when we did, she was always fully dressed and made-up. Today she sat wrapped in a deep mauve dressing gown trimmed with white lace. Her dyed-mahogany hair was hidden in a turban. And—shocker of shockers—she wore no makeup.

"Oh! Good morning!" I said.

"Yes, I know, I know. I feel the way I look," she said drily, tapping her teaspoon lightly against the china cup and laying it down in the saucer. "At my age, beauty sleep is of utmost importance. But bad dreams are keeping me awake. I don't like the energy in the house. Something is amiss."

I opened a cabinet and grabbed a bowl. As I poured out my cereal, I thought about the weird, creepy dream I'd had just before waking up. It was the first time I had dreamed about the white-haired lady, but I had definitely been having odd, fragmented, vaguely frightening dreams for a while now. Lady Azura had been talking about her bad dreams for weeks too. So far I had hesitated to mention my dreams to her, but maybe it was time.

And I felt the strange energy in the house too. Lady Azura had been teaching me to listen to all my senses, and while I'm not totally sure what that means, I have noticed lately that I can kind of pick up on vibes some-times. And the vibes in our house were different lately. But somehow I wasn't as bothered by it as Lady Azura was. Maybe it was because my birthday was coming up, so it was hard for me to stay in a gloomy mood.

I always looked forward to my birthday, with an irrational, little-kid excitement that I really ought to have grown out of by this point. Maybe it was because my dad was the same way. His birthday is in June, and we've always done something really fun on each other's big day. Last year I got to take the day off from school, and we went deep-sea fishing. We hadn't caught anything, which I was secretly relieved about, but we'd seen whales. My dad brought a cooler onto the boat with lunch, and then he surprised me with a little cake, with candles and everything, in the middle of the ocean. That was one of my happiest days I could remember before I moved to New Jersey. I had been wondering what we would do this year to celebrate.

Lady Azura's voice pulled me out of my reverie. "Have you been feeling it too, Sara? The negative energy?"

The white-haired woman's face was etched in my memory. I paused, midway through slicing my banana onto my cereal. "Well, actually, yeah. Kind of. Just last night—"

We heard a loud crash in the hallway outside the kitchen. The sound of breaking glass.

I dropped the rest of my banana beside my bowl. I bounded across the kitchen in three steps and banged open the swinging kitchen door.

"Stay back!"

It was my dad. He was standing frozen in the

hallway, in the midst of at least three broken picture frames. They'd fallen off the wall and shattered.

"There's lots of broken glass," he said.

"I have shoes on," I said, pointing to my Converses and turning back toward the kitchen. "I'll grab the broom. You stay there so you don't track any little pieces of glass."

I guess I must have sounded take-charge and convincing, because he did as I ordered and stayed put.

Lady Azura had risen from her chair and walked toward the kitchen doorway in her high-heeled mule slippers. She peered down the hall at my dad, her brow furrowed. I couldn't tell whether it was a look of concern or annoyance. I was used to reading her face when it was fully made-up.

"What happened?" she demanded of my dad, as I gently edged past her, carrying the broom, dustpan, and kitchen garbage can.

"I don't know," said my dad, taking the broom from me and shooing me away. "I'll take care of this," he said to me. "Go finish breakfast."

I ignored him and carefully stooped down to pick up the large pieces of glass, which I dropped into the bin.

"I was just walking down the hall—careful, honey—thinking about the presentation I have to give today," he said. "And the pictures seemed to jump off the wall. I don't think I even touched them. Maybe it was the vibrations from my footsteps?"

Lady Azura's frown deepened.

"I'm going to be late if I don't get a move on," my dad said, glancing at his watch. "Are you sure you can clean this up, Sara? Are you okay on time before school?"

"It's fine, Dad. Go. Good luck with your presentation!" I said, looking up from the floor to give him a quick smile. Lady Azura had retreated back to the kitchen.

A few seconds after the front door had closed, I heard another crash. This time it was a thud, heavy footsteps, and then the sound of my father saying a bad word. Before I had time to react, the front door slammed back open.

My father stood there, breathing heavily. Now it was his turn to have an annoyed look on his face.

"Whatever is the matter now, Mike?" asked Lady Azura. I heard a slight hint of exasperation in her tone. Evidently my father did too.

"I just tripped over the front porch chair, which *someone* left directly in the way," he growled in an angry voice I seldom heard him use.

Lady Azura sniffed haughtily. "Well, I certainly didn't leave the chair there, if that is what you are implying."

My dad held up a paperback book. One of Lady Azura's romance novels. "This was on the chair," he said, placing it on the table next to the door.

Maybe you shouldn't be such a bull in a china shop.

I'd heard what Lady Azura was thinking.

I hope you aren't getting forgetful. First sign of senility, maybe?

I'd heard that, too. My dad's thoughts.

My head started to throb. It was too early in the morning to listen to family drama.

"I might get stuck working late again and may not be back until after supper's over tonight," my father said as he closed the front door.

I hastily finished sweeping up and tied up the bag. I was going to be late to meet Lily at this rate. I grabbed my backpack, then picked up the garbage bag and headed out the door. "Bye!" I yelled. "I'll grab something to eat at school!"

I heard a muffled reply from Lady Azura in the kitchen.

After dumping the garbage into the bin, I hurried down the front pathway and turned onto Seagate Drive to meet Lily.

I glanced quickly back at the house. It looked the same. The weathered gables. Pale-yellow siding with burnt-orange trim. The huge covered porch. I caught a glimpse of two of the spirits—our spirits, the ones that belonged in my house. The old woman sitting on the porch, knitting. And a young boy in a cap, scampering around on an upstairs balcony. Everything looked the same as it always did. But I couldn't help sharing Lady Azura's feeling that something was not right.

I thought about how I, too, hadn't been the same recently. My ability to read people's thoughts had grown stronger in the past few weeks. I wasn't at all sure that this was a good thing. It made me feel guilty to hear what people were thinking. Like I was eaves-dropping. Intruding. What would be next? X-ray vision? So I could see them in their underwear?

I wondered if my powers were strengthening because I was getting older. I thought about how awful it would be if someone else could read *my* thoughts. I often had fears, or annoyed feelings about other people, that passed quickly. But what if someone tapped into my mind at the very moment I was thinking something terrible?

Lately I felt like I worried all the time. In addition to worrying about my new power, I worried a lot about my dad and Lady Azura. Things had been really tense between them lately.

I was beginning to think Lady Azura was right when she said the energy in the house was bad. What I didn't know, though, was what to do about it.

Chapter 3

Lily was actually there waiting for me as I arrived in front of her house. I must really have been running late, because Lily is almost never waiting somewhere before I am. She's "chronically tardy," as some of our teachers like to say. She was practicing her ballet leaps across the sidewalk, her long brown braid flapping behind her.

"Hey, you!" she shouted as I approached. "How does my cabriole look? I've been working on it!"

I grinned. "Awesome. Probably even more awesome if I actually knew what a cabby-whatever actually is."

She rolled her eyes and linked arms with me, panting slightly from all that jumping around. "Come on. We have to get moving! Do you realize you are actually late, missy? That might be a first for you."

"Yeah, sorry. Lots of drama in the house this morning. Don't ask."

She laughed. "Multiply that times five and you have *my* house this morning."

Lily had three brothers and a sister. And more cousins than I could count on my fingers and toes.

"So. We have to talk. About Saturday," said Lily as we turned onto Ocean Grove Road.

My heart sank. I hoped she wasn't going to suggest having some huge birthday party for me.

"What *about* Saturday?" I asked warily.

"I was talking with Miranda and Avery," she said, "and we were thinking about throwing a big party."

"Oh, now, Lil, hold on. I don't—"

"For Jayden."

That stopped me. I blinked at her.

"Oh! For . . . Jayden?"

"Yeah, because he'll be leaving just after spring break, and I guess there's no other time to have a going-away party before he leaves, because he has so many relatives to go see and stuff. So we thought Saturday would be the perfect night for it."

"Um, yeah. That sounds great," I said.

We walked in silence for a few minutes. The warm March breeze smelled salty and hinted at summer. The leaves were just starting to bud on the trees. I thought about Jayden. He'd told me he was moving to Atlanta when we were at the semiformal dance a few weeks back. Well, actually I'd read his thoughts first. And *then* he'd told me.

Jayden was my first-ever boyfriend. My first-ever kiss. On the cheek, but still. No one knew about the kiss except Lily . . . and Jayden and I, of course. As first boyfriends go, I thought I had definitely won the coolest-first-boyfriend prize. He was really cute, with shaggy brown hair and big brown eyes. Skin the color of caramel. Athletic. Funny. Nice. And I didn't feel shy when I was with him, which was how I usually felt with practically everyone else. He made me laugh. He seemed to genuinely like hanging out with me. So of course I was upset that he was leaving. Of course it made sense to throw a party. But still. It was a little confusing. Did Lily forget Saturday was my birthday?

"Is there, uh, anything I can do? To help with the party?" I asked. I felt awkward asking. Like I was butting in or something.

"Nah, I think we're all set," she said. "It's going to be at Scoops. Uncle Paul even said he'd close it for us specially, so we could have the place all to ourselves, which is pretty awesome." She bounded down the sidewalk, skipping a square of sidewalk with every leap.

"That *is* awesome," I agreed, trotting to catch up with her. We passed a bunch of closed storefronts. My backpack bounced uncomfortably on my back. It seemed to be a rule that all middle-school textbooks had to weigh at least ten pounds each.

We walked in silence for a minute or so. Should I say something? I decided I would.

I tried to make my voice sound as casual as I could. "Oh, and by the way, it's, um, well, Saturday is my birthday. No big deal or anything, but just thought I'd mention it."

Lily stopped leaping, her arms windmilling so she wouldn't fall forward. She smacked her brow and turned to me. "Oh. Jeez," she said. "I totally forgot! I am the worst friend ever!"

"No, you're not. Really, that's fine," I said quickly. And I meant it. At least, I thought I did. The last thing I wanted was a big party for *me*.

But she shook her head and waved her hands, looking really annoyed at herself. "How did I forget your birthday? Lame, lame, lame. Well, we should at least sing 'Happy Birthday' to you."

"No, no, do not. *So* not a big deal. You should make the party about Jayden. I don't want my birthday to be a big event when the party is about him."

Lily looked at me for a moment and then nodded, looking reassured. We resumed our fast-paced walk-trot to school. We were almost there. Lines of buses parked in the semicircular driveway disgorged kids, who streamed up the stairs and into the building through the wide double doors.

"Yeah, I guess that makes sense," she said finally. "But here's what I'll do. How about if we ask some of the gang if they can meet at Scoops on Sunday afternoon? Just a little get-together, no big deal or anything. We won't even call it a birthday celebration or anything."

I smiled. "Sure. That sounds great." But I felt a little let down. Part of me was happy Lily wanted to do *something* for my birthday, but another part of me felt a little disappointed that my birthday didn't seem like a bigger deal to her. I mean, I know I said I didn't want it to be a big deal, and I meant it . . . but I meant it in terms of everyone else. Shouldn't it be a kind of big deal to Lily, my best friend?

But I had no clue about how normal kids celebrated normal birthdays with their friends. Being in a friendship group like this was still new to me. What did I know? I asked myself. Maybe this was just the way people did birthdays around here. I felt a little ashamed of myself for doubting Lily.

Suddenly Lily's thoughts cut into mine. I could hear them.

. . . so much to think about for the party on Saturday . . . hope the Sunday thing satisfies her . . .

Quickly I forced myself to block her thoughts. I squeezed my eyes closed and pushed them away, almost like I was creating a force field around myself.

It actually worked. Her thoughts faded.

"Hey, you okay?" asked Lily, her dark-brown eyes wide with concern. "You look like you're trying to blow up a balloon or something. Your eyes are scrunched up, and your face is all red."

I realized I had been holding my breath. I let it out

quickly. I had to learn how to do this without making a spectacle of myself.

"I-I'm fine," I panted.

And then we heard the first bell. We hustled inside.

In social studies I couldn't find my report about the gold rush. I was positive I'd put it into my binder the night before. But it wasn't there.

Even though I knew it was pointless, I conducted a frantic search through every inch of my backpack. Then inside my textbooks. It wasn't there.

I'm one of these semi-geeky types who never *doesn't* do my homework, so not being able to find my homework puts me in a state of panic.

"Problem, Sara?" Mr. Blake was suddenly looming over my desk.

I stopped frantically rummaging and gave him a helpless shrug. "I'm sorry. I can't find my report. I could have sworn I put it in there last night, but now it's missing."

"Not to worry. Bring it in before first period tomorrow," he said, and moved on to the next desk.

Oh, puh-leese. Can you say "teacher's pet"? If anyone

else in the class had forgotten their report, Blake would
have taken off ten points at least.

I jumped. It had been Miranda's voice. But not her
spoken voice. Her thoughts-inside-her-head voice. I
was learning to hear the difference.

I leaned forward to look at her. She was sitting two
desks away, with Lily in between us. She just raised
her eyebrows and grinned at me, friend to friend, as if
to say, *Whew, that was a close one!* But now that I knew
what she really thought, could I see a hint of dislike
and phoniness behind her smile? I mustered a weak
smile back at her. Inside I was stung.

I leaned back in my chair and stared straight ahead.
I definitely wasn't liking this new skill of mine, the
ability to read minds. Not one bit.

At lunch I plunked down my tray just in time to hear
Avery and Lily talking about a party.

The party.

"So, um, what time is this party for Jayden?" I
asked.

"It's supposed to start at seven thirty, but you should
come over to my house before," said Lily. "Maybe you

can help my mom with the baking, since you're so artistic? Oh, and it's not a surprise or anything. Jayden knows about it."

"That's good," I said. "He doesn't seem like the type who'd enjoy a surprise party."

"Oh, and speaking of parties," said Lily, leaning forward and addressing the whole table. "Did you guys know that it's Sara's birthday on Saturday?"

Some "ohs" and "reallys" chorused around the table. I nodded and shrugged, feeling a little awkward.

"So should we sing 'Happy Birthday' to her on Saturday?" asked Avery. Being talked about like I wasn't sitting right there made me feel *really* awkward.

"No, no, no," said Lily quickly. "Sara told me she doesn't want us to fuss *at all* about her birthday, right, Sara?"

I nodded almost imperceptibly. I was afraid to say something for fear of sounding like I really did mind. Because I wasn't sure *what* I thought. Was it silly that my feelings were hurt?

"And she knows that this party is all about Jayden, and she doesn't want to make it about her. So I was thinking maybe some of you guys might be able to get together at Scoops on Sunday afternoon? To celebrate Sara's birthday. Except we won't even mention that it *is* her birthday, right, Sara? We'll just get together again and hang out a little, totally unofficial. . . ."

This get-together was sounding lamer by the minute.

"Because she hates being the center of attention and all that," Lily finished with a smile in my direction.

Avery's thoughts lasered into my mind.

As IF! And miss hanging out with my cousin and his dreamy friends for ice cream with a bunch of girls?

"I am soooo sorry, Sara," Avery said, out loud this time. "But my family already switched our plans from Saturday to Sunday because of Jayden's party. I have to go visit my cousins on Sunday. I would so rather celebrate your birthday, but I promised my mom."

Wow. Avery had just said practically the exact opposite of what she'd thought. How could she do that? I sat back and nodded, feeling numb. "That's fine," I said. "I understand."

I didn't want to have to hear other people's thoughts. What they really thought, that is. Did everyone do this? Say one thing and think another? Did *I* do that?

I pretended to drop my spoon on the floor so I could put up my clumsy blocking technique while I was under the table, where no one would see me. Below the edge of the table, I squeezed my eyes shut. Willed an invisible bubble to form around me, so others' thoughts would bounce off and not make their way inside my head.

"I'll try to make it," said Marlee vaguely.

"I don't know if I can," said Tamara. "I might have to babysit for my little brother."

I had to sit back up sometime. "That's fine, you guys. I know the Saturday party is a lot of effort and stuff," I mumbled. *Don't cry. Don't cry.* That was the voice inside my own head. I swallowed the huge lump that had risen in the back of my throat.

Lily looked at me, concern written all over her face. "You okay, Sar?" she asked in a soft voice.

"I'm great!" I said as cheerfully as I possibly could. I knew I was being a big baby. I was definitely feeling extra emotional because Jayden was leaving. Or maybe I was just extremely immature about the fact that no one seemed to care that it was my birthday. What did I expect? The days of princess dresses and pink frosted cakes and balloons and pin-the-tail-on-the-donkey were past me. It was time to grow up. And last year, in California, I didn't have one friend to wish me a happy birthday. This year I had a table full of friends making excuses about why they couldn't hang out for my birthday. That was an improvement of sorts, right?

Suddenly Jayden appeared at the table.

"Hey, dudes!" he said cheerfully to everyone at my table. "Talking about the par-tay?"

"Yep," said Lily. "We're trying to decide between throwing your party at the Ritz or jetting everyone to the Riviera."

He grinned. "Cool. Both sound awesome. So, can you come on Saturday?" he asked me.

"Well, I had something way more important to do, but I canceled. I wouldn't miss it for the world," I said, making my voice come out a lot more lighthearted and cheerful than I was actually feeling at that moment.

His smile widened. Then he moved along to the next table, where most of the boys from the basketball team usually sat together.

As if I needed more problems at that moment, I

suddenly heard a loud voice bellow my name from across the cafeteria.

"Collins! I need to talk to you pronto!"

I stifled a groan and looked around for an escape route. Now was not the time for me to have a conversation with the long-dead spirit of a school gym teacher.

"Right now! On the double! Move it, Collins!"

My number one life goal at my new school was to fit in. To look normal. Having the entire school see me talking to thin air was probably not the best way to look normal. Now would definitely be a good time to leave the cafeteria.

I stood up. "Got to get to the library to print something before English," I said.

I bussed my tray, then hurried for the door, ignoring the gym teacher as he continued to bellow my name from across the noisy room.

Chapter 4

I rushed home from school, anxious to talk to Lady Azura. I was so over this mind-reading stuff. I wanted her to teach me a way to turn it off for good. I was sure she would know how. She always seemed to have the answers to questions I had. Sometimes she even knew the answer before I'd figured out what the question would be. I often had trouble understanding what she actually meant, though. She tended to speak in riddles.

The first thing I saw when I opened the front door was my history report. Sitting right on the front-hall table. Before I could react to why it was there, and how it had gotten there, I smelled something very wrong.

It smelled like smoke.

Well, not exactly like smoke from a fire that was burning. It wasn't the same sort of smoke I'd smelled that awful night a few weeks ago, when there had been an actual fire, upstairs, in the pink bedroom. This was a *smoky* smell. Like from an old campfire or something.

Still, even if nothing was actively burning, this smell couldn't be a good thing. Something *had* been burning.

There was no sign of Lady Azura. But the door to her summoning room was closed. That meant she most likely had a client. And the smoky smell was coming from the sitting room across the hall. I strode over and stopped short in the doorway, surveying the room. My mouth dropped open in horror, then immediately closed again, because I began coughing uncontrollably.

It wasn't smoke. It was soot. Dirty clouds of soot. Soot billowed out of the chimney. It coated every surface in the room. It looked as though a downdraft was blowing the ashes in the wrong direction. Rather than going up the chimney, they were coming down, through the open damper, and ashes were shooting into the room.

I dashed into the room, trying not to breathe, and stooped down to try to jimmy the damper closed. I got a face full of soot for my efforts. But after some jiggling and shifting around, I managed to get the thing closed. Black soot completely covered my hand.

Coughing and sputtering, I ran out of the room and closed the French doors we never closed. I was grateful they were there.

I was still standing there, my back to the door, my elbow raised to my face, coughing and wheezing, when the door to Lady Azura's room opened, and a large woman with red hair emerged. She barely glanced my way. She did not look very pleased.

"My new blouse is ruined!" she said over her shoulder.

I noticed a brown, blotchy stain down the front of her blouse.

Lady Azura stood and leaned in the doorway, her arms crossed. She tossed her head haughtily but did not respond until the woman had slammed the front door behind her.

"I did you a favor!" Lady Azura called after the woman, although of course the woman couldn't possibly have heard. "That blouse was hideous!" She tipped her chin up and shrugged and then spoke, as if to herself. "She didn't like what I had to tell her. Sometimes the truth hurts." Suddenly she sniffed. Looked my way. She seemed to notice me for the first time, standing with my back to the doors of the sitting room.

"The tea leaves spilled down her blouse. I did nothing. They simply leaped from the cup." She furrowed her brow. "What is that dreadful smell? Why on earth are you standing there? And what is smeared all over your face?"

"Ashes," I said. "There seems to be a problem with the chimney in the sitting room."

I opened the doors and gestured toward the room. A small puff of soot unfurled from the room as I did so.

She stared into the room. Her brown eyes, heavily ringed with black eyeliner and thick black eyelashes, widened with surprise and dismay.

"What a state the room is in! We must clean it up, Sara. Why don't you fetch the broom and vacuum? I'll go change."

Ten minutes later, she reappeared. My eyes widened at the sight of her wearing velvet sweatpants and a T-shirt advertising an old Broadway show I'd never heard of. Her hair was tucked up into a pink turban. I suppressed a smile. Lady Azura in leisure wear. I wished for a moment that Lily was here to see this.

For the next hour and a half, we dusted, swept, and vacuumed. We pounded a couple of small throw rugs on the clothesline outside.

Coughing, opening windows, setting up fans to try to get rid of the worst of the sooty smell, we didn't say much.

After we finally finished, the room looked a lot better. It seemed to smell better too, but by that time our noses were so used to it they were probably immune. Luckily, both of the couches had washable slipcovers, which meant we could have them cleaned to get rid of the smell and stuff. I balled them up and stuffed them into large yard bags so my dad could take them to the dry cleaner.

"I believe the next step is for both of us to bathe," said Lady Azura, staring at me with a glimmer of amusement in her eyes. She was right. Much of the soot seemed to have transferred from the room to ourselves. It was funny to see her in a state of disarray, when she was always so beautifully dressed and groomed.

"Go. Have a luxurious bath or shower, my dear," commanded Lady Azura. "I will do the same. Then we'll talk."

In the shower, I scrubbed my body with a washcloth. I had to wash my hair three times before the water that swirled down the drain ran clear. And I thought the smell of soot would never leave my nose. But an hour later, Lady Azura and I sat down to a quiet dinner of spinach salad together. Knowing that a salad would not be enough for me, Lady Azura thoughtfully placed a platter of warm cornbread in front of me.

"Your father is working late," she told me. "Perhaps now might be a good time for us to compare notes. About the house. The negative energy that we both feel." She locked eyes with me.

Did she think I knew something she didn't? I paused in the middle of buttering a big slab of cornbread. "It does seem like weird stuff has been happening," I ventured finally, when it was clear she was going to make me speak first. "Like my dad and those pictures crashing down. The chair on the porch. The teacup that spilled by itself on that lady. And now the chimney thing in the front room." I shrugged.

"Yes. I believe that most of those events are outside of the ordinary."

"And also we're both having weird dreams."

She looked at me sharply. "Are *you* having weird dreams as well, Sara?"

"Well, sort of. This morning when I woke up I thought it was still dark out, but then I thought there was this dark cloud over my bed. Maybe I dreamed it, I don't know."

Dark cloud! Is she mistaken?

"No, I don't think so," I said.

I realized too late that she hadn't asked me that question out loud. I'd just heard what she was thinking.

I heard her breathe in sharply.

I avoided her gaze and concentrated on cutting my cornbread into neat little pieces.

Lady Azura stood up slowly from the table. I jumped up to clear away the dinner stuff.

"Leave that," she said. "Come. To my room. Now."

I knew it was pointless to argue. Luckily, it was a light homework night. I followed her out of the kitchen, down the hall, and into her fortune-telling room.

She sat down at her round table and beckoned me to sit across from her.

I sat down warily, wondering if I was in trouble. I hadn't mentioned to her about my new ability to read people's minds. What if she got mad at me for not saying anything? The reason I hadn't said anything was that the power had sort of come on gradually. The first few times I'd overheard other people's thoughts, I hadn't even been sure that's what was happening.

She rested her elbows on the table and clasped her hands. She seemed unsure of where to begin. Finally she leaned toward me. "Has anything changed for you in the past few weeks?"

I wasn't sure what to say. I suddenly felt apprehensive about talking to her about this. What if she got angry at me for reading *her* thoughts? I tried to focus on her thoughts, to see if she was angry with me, but I drew a blank. She probably knew how to put up a blockade or something.

"Um, well, yeah," I stammered out. "I have definitely had some weird stuff happen. Strange dreams, like I already mentioned."

She nodded. "You should keep a notepad near your

bed. Write down any strange dreams you have, so you remember the details, and then we can discuss them."

"Okay," I said. "And there's been some other strange stuff too." I told her about my missing homework. About Lily being so casual about my birthday. About Jayden moving away.

Lady Azura's face relaxed. She smiled sympathetically. Nodded. And then all of a sudden I could hear her thoughts.

Just the usual adolescent silliness, thank goodness.

I jumped as though I'd been stung.

She thought my problems were silly. Not important. First Lily, now my great-grandmother. Twice in one day, my feelings had been hurt by people I cared most about.

Lady Azura hadn't noticed my response, because she had already stood up and gone over to the sideboard. She opened her drawer and began rummaging around. She turned toward me, holding out a small crystal. It was green and sort of twirly and bubbly inside. I stared at it. It had a beautiful pattern, like deep lake water that swirls around a boat's oars.

"This is a moldavite crystal," she said, placing the

green stone into my outstretched hand. "It will protect you from the negative energy in the house. It is a stone of intense frequency and high vibration."

I blinked at her. I had no idea what she was talking about.

"It is a powerful, protective stone. Negative entities find it difficult to latch on to your aura when you wear it. I have one as well."

It was a really pretty stone. I attached it to the cord around my neck. I felt its weight against my collarbone. It felt warm, and—this was weird—like it was ever so slightly *vibrating* against my skin. Faint but detectable.

Lady Azura looked around the room distractedly, as though she'd forgotten I was still there.

"Well, so, thanks," I said. A little stiffly maybe. I was still a little hurt about the "adolescent silliness" comment. Actually, not comment—thought. Which, when I reflected on it, wasn't very fair. Didn't I often have thoughts that weren't very nice? She hadn't *said* it to me.

I wanted to know more about this "negative energy" she kept talking about. I kept thinking there was more to the story than Lady Azura was letting on. It bothered me that she was keeping it from me. As though trying to protect me. Did she think I couldn't deal with it?

I was finishing the washing up in the kitchen when I finally heard my father's truck in the driveway. I glanced at the clock. Nearly eight thirty. Lady Azura had retired to her room. I could hear her watching her favorite miniseries, some British drama about a bunch of people living in a huge manor house and getting all dressed up for dinner every night.

I was just opening the refrigerator to take out the pitcher of iced tea for my dad when I heard the crash.

So hard the house shook.

With my heart in my throat and a sick feeling in my stomach, I raced to the door to see what had happened.

Chapter 5

My father had driven his truck into the garage.

The garage was really an old carriage house. Lady Azura told me it had been built long before cars were invented. But it was big enough to hold two cars. Darkness had set in by now, but by some miracle, the headlights hadn't gone out. I could see debris and falling plaster still raining down onto the top of his truck. I could also see that the airbag had inflated, and that he was moving inside, shimmying out of the driver's-side door.

I sprinted to the garage just as my dad emerged, looking shaken but unhurt.

"Are you okay?" I asked, running over to give him a hug.

He hugged me back and nodded. "I'm fine,

kiddo. But I have no idea how that just happened," he said, brushing white powder off first one arm, then the other. Then out of his hair. "The accelerator malfunctioned. I was pulling in, ever so slowly, and then the gas pedal seemed to depress to the floor all by itself."

I nodded, hugely relieved that he was okay, but full of new anxiety. What was happening to this house? Was some sort of bad spirit causing these things to happen?

Lady Azura's car didn't seem like it had been damaged. She kept a tarp over it because she so rarely used it. But on the side where my dad parked his truck, I could see cracks all up and down the back wall.

"I'll have a look tomorrow, when it's light out," he said, wearily leading me into the house. "Looks like there's going to be some front-end damage. And the garage will need some serious repairs. There goes *my* weekend." He was muttering now, half to himself.

"Gracious me, Mike, what on earth happened out there?" asked Lady Azura as she hurried into the kitchen.

"Little mishap with the accelerator," he said. "I'm

fine, but the truck will need to be towed to Vern's tomorrow."

Lady Azura and I exchanged a look. Her expression said, *Another little mishap?*

"Hoping I can borrow the ocean liner for the day," he said, missing our silent exchange.

"Of course, of course," murmured Lady Azura.

Underneath that tarp, Lady Azura kept a huge, powder-blue convertible from the fifties that still ran. It had wide tail fins jutting up in the back and pearly whitewall tires. I'd only seen her drive it once since we'd gotten here, and that was to visit a friend for tea who lived two blocks away. Watching her turn onto the main road did sort of remind me of the way an ocean liner makes a turn—slowly, grandly, and with a very wide arc. My dad told me the car was in near-perfect condition.

My father set down his briefcase and sniffed the air suspiciously. "What happened here? Has there been another fire?"

"Oh, nothing to be concerned about," said Lady Azura casually. "Just a bit of back-draft from the chimney. I am sure the chimney just needs to be relined and cleaned. And who knows what sort of birds are nesting up there. Sara and I did a bit of vacuuming, and it's all taken care of now." She glanced at me, and I read her look: *Let's not make a big deal of this,* her expression told me.

My dad eyed her suspiciously. His face had a weird, ghostly look to it, because it had a fine layer of white powder on it—from the airbag going off, I knew. But I could read his expression, too. He looked like he didn't believe a word she'd said. I didn't want to hear his thoughts. I tried to put up the bubble, but I guess I was too tired. It dropped the second his thoughts hit it, and they came streaming into my mind.

First the fire upstairs. Now this. The place is a firetrap. We've got to find somewhere else to live. Maybe I can convince her to sell this place. . . .

I knew he was worried, after the fire we'd had a few weeks ago in the upstairs pink bedroom. But I couldn't believe he would really make us move. This was our *home.* The first place I had ever been really happy in. What would I do if he really decided we had to leave?

My worried state grew so bad my breathing became shallow. My skin went dry. My heart thumped. Was I having an anxiety attack or something?

"I'm going upstairs to shower," my dad said, and trudged up the steps.

"I guess I'll head up and do my homework," I said to Lady Azura in a quivery voice.

She looked at me strangely. One of those searching, sharp looks that made me feel like she could see straight through me.

"You've had a long day, " she said finally. "And you bear greater burdens than most children your age. Get some rest. Try to think positive thoughts before you fall asleep, Sara. That, combined with the crystal I gave you, will hopefully grant you a good night's rest without bad dreams." With that she gave me a gentle squeeze on the shoulder and then headed to her room. I watched her retreating back, my anxiety soothed somewhat for the moment, and then turned and headed up to my own room.

Up in my room I tried to relax. I did try to think positive thoughts, but I was too preoccupied. So I tried to study my English vocab for the quiz I had the next day. But the words just swam in front of my eyes. Finally I gave up. I put down my note cards and crawled into bed.

Either the crystal was faulty, which I doubted, or the house was just too full of bad energy, because my sleep was plagued with bad dreams. I kept waking up with my heart pounding but couldn't remember what I'd dreamed about. Lady Azura had told me to record my dreams with a pen and pad next to my bed. I tried to scribble a few things on the pad before falling back asleep. When the alarm went off the next morning, I felt like I had barely slept a wink. In a daze I looked at the pad where I had jotted down notes about my dreams, and it looked like I'd written in Chinese. I couldn't read a thing I'd scrawled in the darkness.

I stumbled blearily through my morning routine. Showering, dressing, brushing my teeth, looking longingly at the rumpled covers on my bed, inviting me to crawl back underneath and snooze just one more minute. But I resisted. I grabbed my backpack off the floor and headed downstairs.

I felt exhausted as I walked into the kitchen. And this time I was not surprised to find Lady Azura sitting at the breakfast table. She looked as though she'd been up for a while, and that she'd had the same sort of bad-dream-filled night I had had. But at least this morning she was fully dressed in a silky, swirly blouse and shimmery skirt, and fully made-up with heavily lined eyes, greenish-shadowed eyelids, bright-pink lipstick.

My dad was just setting her teacup and saucer in front of her. She nodded slightly, looking distracted, far away in her own thoughts.

"Morning," I mumbled to both of them, moving slowly to the refrigerator for the milk. "More bad dreams last night?"

"Yes," she said. "This is getting quite tiresome."

I nodded. "Me too." I set down the milk and rubbed my face with the palms of my hands, trying to get the circulation moving. Like my great-grandmother, I'm not much of a morning person.

"Well, I can outdo the both of you," my dad said grimly. He stood at the counter, buttering a thick slice of toast for himself. "I didn't bother with bad dreams. I just stayed awake half the night, fretting."

"About what?" I asked cautiously.

I heard his thoughts.

Car. Work. House. Money.

"Car. Work. House. Money. Whether I won the lottery, even though I didn't actually buy a lottery ticket," he said, grinning at me. "The usual grown-up stuff."

At least his thoughts and his words were consistent. More than I could say for some of my friends from school. And I was relieved to see his grin. Maybe he wasn't that worried if he still had a sense of humor.

"I've called Vern Randazzo," said my dad. "He'll be by for the truck midmorning sometime."

Vern was the town's only mechanic, but my dad said he was reasonable and honest. No surprise there. Vern was yet another of Lily's relatives. I think a great-uncle on her dad's side, but I wasn't positive.

I'd been wondering what we were going to do about my birthday. It was three days away, and neither of them had said a word about it, at least recently. I wondered if they even remembered. I told myself to get over it. The self-pity thing was annoying even to myself.

"Oh, by the way," I said casually, pouring milk over my cereal. "Is it okay if I go to a party Saturday night? At Scoops?"

I waited for one of them to ask if it was a birthday

party. For me. But all my dad said was, "Uh, sure. Sounds good."

I looked over at Lady Azura. She was glowering down at her tea, as though waiting for it to explain to her why she was up at such an early hour.

I tuned in to their thoughts. I heard my dad's first.

Thank goodness the most important thing Sara has to think about is an upcoming party.

Then Lady Azura's.

Ah, youth. To be able to distract oneself so easily with the thoughts of a party.

I blocked them both. This time it came easily. Why couldn't I figure out how to do it consistently?

Irritation boiled up inside me. Did they think I was shallow? That my only thoughts were about parties? That I didn't feel some of the worry and stress that our family was dealing with?

Maybe it was lack of sleep. Or worry about this bad new direction my powers seemed to be taking. Whatever it was, my anger flared up. I decided to come right out with it.

"So. In case you forgot, which you seem to have done, I thought I would remind you both that Saturday is my birthday." I fought back angry tears.

My dad swirled around, his mouth full of toast. "Totally spaced on that for a minute, kiddo," he said, swallowing quickly. "But of course I knew it was your birthday. I just forgot for a minute there."

Lady Azura closed her eyes and let out a long sigh. "My dear, I did not forget your birthday. But as you know, morning is not my best time of day. Forgive an old woman a temporary memory lapse."

I stared at the floor. I felt bad that I'd been so immature. But my feelings were still hurt from over-hearing their thoughts. "It's okay," I mumbled. What was wrong with me? I'd been so irritable and anxious the past few weeks. Maybe it *was* the negative energy Lady Azura kept talking about.

"So the party on Saturday is for you?" asked my dad as he loaded his cup and dish into the dishwasher and glanced at his watch.

"Actually, no. It's for a kid at school who's moving away," I said. My dad knew who Jayden was, of course, because we'd gone to the semiformal together, and he'd met him at our Halloween party last fall, but he probably didn't remember. I mean, he tried to be involved with my life, but I wasn't the kind of kid who shared every little detail. Like how Jayden and I were sort-of-kind-of going out.

Lady Azura seemed to rally. She looked up from her tea and smiled at me. "Well, I'm glad you have a party to go to, my dear," she said. "Perhaps we can celebrate your birthday on a different day."

"Yeah! That's a good idea!" said my dad. He looked relieved that I had something to do. Had he made *plans* on my birthday? Had he asked someone out on a date or something? He definitely had a guilty look on his face. "Maybe the three of us can go out to dinner next weekend."

I focused back in on my dad's thoughts, to see what he was really thinking. Had he really forgotten that it was his only child's birthday? But all I got were scrambled thoughts. *Work, car, money, house.* His mind seemed to be a whirlwind of incoherent snippets. I tried Lady Azura again. But this time she was unreadable.

I tried not to show how let down I felt. It was just a dumb birthday.

Chapter 6

I slept badly again that night. My dreams were restless. I kept waking up, nagged by worries. An unnamed distress loomed over me. I tossed and turned. Felt powerless. Frightened. I clutched the covers closer and rolled over, trying to get back to sleep.

And then I dreamed about the woman from the boardwalk again.

This dream was as vivid as the other one had been. Not jumbled up like my other dreams.

This time, though, she wasn't on the boardwalk. She was in our house. Standing next to Lady Azura's table, handing her something.

I was right there in the room with them. Over near the window. But neither one seemed to know I was there. Maybe they couldn't see me, because the heavy shades were slightly open, and I was backlit by the sun. It was the weirdest dream. It seemed so crystal clear. As though it were really happening.

"Take it." The woman practically spat the words.

Lady Azura looked troubled. Unusual for her. She always seemed so confident. It was unnerving to see her like this, even though I knew it was a dream.

"Please keep it," Lady Azura said to the woman. She made no effort to take the object the woman was holding out to her.

I took a step forward to look at the object more closely. Neither of them seemed to see me. I saw with a start that it was a moldavite crystal. Large and green and swirly, a bigger version of the one Lady Azura had given me.

"I tell you, I don't need it," the woman said, thrusting her hand closer toward Lady Azura and giving it a little impatient shake. When Lady Azura did not reach for the crystal, the woman let out an exaggerated sigh of exasperation and dropped it onto the table. The thud made me jump.

I didn't like this woman.

"I want *more* power, not less," the woman snapped. "Do you not understand me?"

Dream or no dream, Lady Azura is not the type of person who reacts well to someone implying she is stupid. She crossed her arms and fixed the woman with her iciest stare. Even though it wasn't directed at me, it made *me* quiver.

"I understand you perfectly," she said.

"Then do you understand the *implications*? The *possibilities*? Already I have catapulted up through the ranks at work. No one can stop me. No one can do what I do. Why would I want to change that?"

Lady Azura sighed. "But at what cost, Nina? At what cost?"

The woman's green eyes blazed. "You're just jealous. You *wish* you could do what I do."

"No, in fact, I do not."

"You're nothing more than a charlatan. With my powers, I could run you out of business in a heartbeat." She laughed unpleasantly. "But not to worry. Carry on with your little game. Give your shoreline tourists a bit of fun. I have set my sights much, much higher."

"I think you should leave," said Lady Azura. Her voice was steely.

The woman turned to leave, but paused at the doorway. She turned around. Stared straight at me. I was so startled, I took a step backward. And crashed through the window.

I screamed.

And woke up.

I opened my eyes. It was the middle of the night. I shivered, still freaked out from the dream. But at the same time I felt drugged with sleepiness. I fought the urge to roll over. Instead I leaned over my bed for the little notebook and pen that I kept on the floor. Blindly scribbling, I made a few notes about the dream, but this time I was awake enough to make an effort to write carefully. The woman with white hair. The crystal. Her conversation. Then I dropped the pen onto the pad and rolled over, sinking almost immediately back into sleep.

I soon drifted into another dream.

This one was much less focused. A series of images. Spoken words. Restless feelings and fragmented scenes. My disappointment about my birthday. Jayden leaving. The indifference of my family, my friends. I was in the cafeteria, sitting at a crowded table, but invisible. People talked over my head, ignored what I said, reached across me for stuff. Then I was home, in the kitchen, but my dad and Lady Azura were both talking, talking, talking on their phones. Lady Azura on the house phone; my dad on his cell phone. Neither seemed to notice I was even sitting there. And then I was sitting in a darkened theater. Watching Lily and Miranda, dancing on a brightly lit stage. I sat watching. Watching them and feeling jealous that they were together, that they shared this special bond.

I sat up quickly in bed, wide awake. That dream sequence had been more troubling than the first one. I decided not to write it down. I didn't want to remember it.

I looked at the clock. A little past three in the morning. The house was still. The moon outside was full, and my room was lit with silver moonbeams.

I had the distinct feeling that I wasn't alone in my room.

My heart thumped. I looked around. The curtain fluttered ever so slightly, even though the window was closed. But they were leaky windows. No doubt a breeze had stirred it. Or was there a spirit in here? That couldn't be. The house spirits, the ones I had come to know and get used to, almost never came into my room.

Gradually I became aware of the cloud.

There was a cloud inside my room. I was sure of it this time.

It seemed to be hovering over my bed. Over me. My throat went dry. My heart raced. All my muscle fibers felt tight. Stressed.

I couldn't help but be reminded of one of those dark rain clouds I used to see in the cartoons, the ones that floated directly above the characters as they drove in a car or whatever, and didn't affect anyone else around them.

I rubbed my eyes. The cloud stayed.

I peered into it. I felt that I had no power to look away. I could see through it, the hazy outline of my ceiling, the patterned, curlicue molding, the familiar crack that zigzagged outward from the corner of the ceiling. I was overcome by an awful wave of fear. Anxiety. It wasn't normal. This cloud shouldn't be here. I felt like I was suffocating, like I desperately needed to claw my way out of this stifling, heavy darkness.

Instinctively, my hand flew to my collarbone. I clutched at the stones that were hanging from my necklace. My fingers searched for the crystal that Lady Azura had just given to me. I put my hand over it and held it tightly. It felt warm and solid in my hand. And it was definitely vibrating. I closed my eyes against the dark cloud. What had she told me to do?

Her words made their way into my muddled mind. "Positive energy. Think positive thoughts."

I began to chant to myself. "I am protected. I am loved. I am strong enough to overcome this." I thought about the people I loved. Who loved me.

And then I thought about my mother. Conjured up my picture of her, the one of her sitting on the rock and laughing. *Help me, Mom,* I wished silently.

I opened my eyes. The cloud was still there, but another cloud, a different cloud, had formed alongside it. The new cloud was silvery. Light. Swirling with sparkly stuff. Was it a reflection of the moonbeams? It reminded me of the way a sunbeam dances with dust motes on a lazy summer afternoon. It brought on a calming feeling. I felt my furrowed forehead slacken, as though the worries were streaming away from me.

The light, silvery cloud moved into the dark cloud, as though the two forces were in opposition. As I watched, the dark cloud moved away from me. It swirled and churned like smoke, and then seemed to thicken and blacken, tumbling around and around. I watched as it swirled and roiled around the room and then seemed to get sucked out of the room, underneath the door.

I wasn't scared anymore. I was mad. I swung my legs out of bed and set out in pursuit. I felt this overwhelming urge to follow it, to keep it from harming my family.

I opened my door. I could see it tumbling down the hall. The cloud stopped in front of my father's closed bedroom door.

Then, from behind me, the silver cloud zoomed out of my room and swirled past me. Was it chasing the dark cloud? It seemed to be. The dark cloud began to dissipate, like smoke from a smoke ring. It glided away and then drifted apart until it vanished.

I had no idea what I had just seen. But the terrible thoughts I'd dreamed about were gone. I no longer felt worried. Or anxious.

I got back into bed and fell asleep.

A deep, dreamless sleep.

The next morning I woke up feeling much better, even though I heard the rain before I opened my eyes.

It was pouring outside. One of those gray, cold, drenching spring rains. But somehow my spirits weren't dampened. I felt lighter and happier than I'd felt in days.

I picked up the notebook next to my bed. This time I could more or less read what I'd scrawled in my dream journal: *Woman with white hair. Crystal. Lady A. mad. Power.*

The dream was still vivid in my memory.

Maybe it was because I had finally gotten a decent night's sleep, but I realized that the dark feeling of anxiety I had been carrying around with me lately seemed to be gone. I felt like me again. I decided I would talk to Lily. Today. About my birthday. Maybe we could do something together tomorrow, just the two of us. I felt sure Lily hadn't intentionally meant to hurt my feelings about my birthday.

Chapter 7

Lily was late that morning. I wondered if she'd overslept because of the rain. I heard on the television once that people are more likely to oversleep on rainy days. That made sense to me. I always had a hard time getting up when it was raining.

I stood by her front walkway, my raincoat hood pulled low down over my eyes and cinched tightly, stomping my feet and aiming my umbrella into the wind in an effort to keep the rain away. That didn't work. It was one of those rains that seem to come from all directions, making the use of an umbrella semi-pointless.

I was just wondering if today would be the day I'd get my very first tardy slip, when Lily finally burst out of her front door and splashed down the path toward me.

"Sorrrrrrreeeeee!" she trilled, struggling to open her umbrella as she ran. "Yucky weather! I could not decide which rain boots to wear!"

The idea that anyone might have more than one pair of rain boots to choose from kind of amazed me. But that was Lily. And sure enough, her pink polka-dotted rain boots looked way better than my boring brown ones. She managed to look great, even in the pouring rain.

I took a flying leap over a puddle, my heavy back-pack bouncing on my back. "Yep. But luckily, it's supposed to clear up by tomorrow." Maybe now was a good time to bring it up. "Hey, speaking of tomorrow, do you, um, feel like hanging out? It doesn't have to be an actual birthday thing or anything like that, but—"

"You cannot believe the drama in my house this morning," said Lily, who seemed not to have heard me. "My brother lost his baseball glove—or at least he thought he did, until he realized he left it out on the lawn overnight and it got rained on, which evidently is the end of the *world*, judging by the way he flipped out this morning."

I waited for her to take a breath and tried again.

"So, tomorrow? I was thinking—"

"And then Cammie decided to try to flush several Super Balls down the toilet. Apparently, she saw someone do this in a cartoon. But they kept bobbing back up, and it wasn't until the third try that . . ."

I tuned out what she was saying. Without really meaning to, I focused in on her thoughts. Was she intentionally trying to change the subject? Her words tumbled out in a steady stream, like coins from a slot machine, making it hard to read her thoughts. I'd never realized it, but when a person is speaking, her thought stream kind of pauses—almost like you can't talk and think at the same time. Anyway, it wasn't easy to hear her thoughts. They came to me in brief snippets during the infrequent pauses in her conversation. But I heard enough.

Tomorrow? Not tomorrow! . . . shopping date with Miranda! Jayden's present! . . . think, think, think . . . need a reason . . . my recital! Aha! Good. Have to practice for my recital . . .

I put up the shield. Managed to tune her out completely now—both what she was saying and what she was thinking. I was stunned. Lily and Miranda were going shopping together? And they were going to chip in to buy Jayden a present? Together? Wasn't he *my* sort-of-kind-of boyfriend? Why were they buying him something? Wasn't it enough that they were throwing him a party? Without asking me for any help?

I tuned back in to her words.

"—so yeah, then my mom was on the phone with the plumber, and it was one of those 'eventful' mornings." She crooked her fingers into air quotes.

She was obviously trying to change the subject. To keep it away from doing something together tomorrow. I didn't know how to feel. Confused? Hurt? Mad? Having a best friend might be all new to me, but I was certain this wasn't normal behavior. Why was Lily treating me like this?

I was pretty quiet for the rest of the walk to school. I swallowed away the huge lump in the back of my throat. My eyes burned, but I didn't cry. Between my hood and my soggy hair, my face was covered, so Lily didn't notice.

I spent the first half of the day going over my conversation with Lily in my mind. Could I have misread something? Or had I done something wrong without realizing it?

At lunch I was still upset. Lily and Miranda were chatting away as I slid into my seat with my tray. I stared down at my taco. I wasn't all that hungry anyway, and what was left of my appetite rapidly vanished as I observed the greasy orange sauce pooling around the taco, and realized it was not even remotely warm. I shoved my tray away a few inches, then opened my milk carton and took a long gulp. The light, normal feeling I'd woken up with was long gone.

"So I guess the Sunday thing didn't work out so well," said Lily, turning to me suddenly. "You know. For your birthday. Are you okay with it?"

"Me? Sure. I mean, whatever," I mumbled.

"I guess it's just a busy weekend," said Lily apologetically. But something in her voice was off. Like she wasn't really all that sorry.

I was aware that the others at the table had turned toward us to listen. I suddenly felt bold. Maybe Lily wouldn't be able to hang out tomorrow, but possibly someone else would.

"Well, hey, how about tomorrow?" I asked.

"Anyone feel like hanging out, maybe going to Scoops or whatever?"

I saw Miranda and Lily exchange a quick look. Marlee suddenly looked very interested in reading the ingredients on her granola bar wrapper. Tamara shoved a heaping forkful of taco into her mouth. Avery coughed.

I started to hear a chorus of their thoughts inside my head, but I forced myself to block them. I didn't want to know.

After an awkward silence, Lily finally spoke. "Sar, I'm so sorry, but we have dinner plans with Aunt Angela and her family tomorrow, and we have to leave early."

Lily was lying. I knew it without having to read her thoughts.

"Okay," I said. I felt my lower lip quivering, but I made it stop. "So I guess you're going to your aunt's *after* you practice for your dance recital, then?"

The stunned look on Lily's face told me I'd gone too far. She looked hurt. Then surprised. And then completely baffled.

With a pang, I realized my mistake. She'd never

said out loud that she had to practice for her recital. She'd only thought it. And I just let her know that I'd heard her thinking it this morning.

Luckily, Tamara changed the subject. "I dropped my Spanish workbook in a puddle this morning," she said. "Anyone have one I can borrow for Spanish class next period?"

I was relieved that the focus had shifted away from my conversation with Lily. I felt completely awful.

My gaze was distracted by a movement across the crowded cafeteria.

It was the spirit of the gym teacher. The one who always seemed to show up at the times I least felt like dealing with him.

"Collins!" he boomed.

Of course, I was the only one who could hear him.

"Need you to do me a favor, Collins! Now, don't you go rushing out on me again! I know your tricks! Hey! Collins!"

"Gotta run," I said to my friends, already standing and turning to hustle out of the cafeteria. "See you, guys."

And I ducked out before the spirit could make

his way toward me. Well, at least I'd managed to do something right. I'd managed to avoid the spirit for one more day.

I was good at avoiding things.

Chapter 8

By the time school was out on Thursday afternoon, the gloomy skies had cleared a little. The sun actually looked as though it was trying to peer out from the light-gray clouds. Puddles were everywhere, though, and I got soaked twice by cars fanning water on me as they whooshed through waterlogged streets.

When I got home, Lady Azura was waiting for me. I peeled off my wet jacket and hung it on a hanger on the inside of the closet door, where it could drip dry without soaking everything around it.

"I've made some tea," she said by way of hello. "Run up and change into dry clothes and I'll pour you a cup."

A few minutes later, I was sitting at the cozy kitchen table, my hair still damp and stringy, but warm again in my comfiest sweats, sipping sweet tea and nibbling on the cookies Lady Azura had put out on a little plate for me. I felt some of the stress of the day melt away.

"Finish your tea," she said as I reached for the last cookie. "Then come into my room. We must meditate together." She stood up and walked out of the kitchen, leaving a trail of exotic scent in her wake.

I had known her long enough to understand that what she really meant was, "Hurry up and finish your tea." So I gulped down one more sip, carried my cup to the sink, and then followed her into her room.

She was already sitting at her table, eyes closed, calmly breathing. She opened one eye and addressed me. "Come. Sit. We'll meditate together and see if we can't rid the house of what is afflicting it."

I sat down warily.

"The negative energy that has invaded this house must be offset by positive energy. I have given this matter much thought, and I believe that if we combine our powers, we can rid the house of this terrible burden."

"Do you know the source of the bad energy?" I asked.

"That's not important," she said. She kept her eyes

closed and hummed. She was avoiding my question. I was sure of it.

I tuned in to her thoughts. I heard a name: *Nina Oliver*. Then, as if a trapdoor had slid closed, I couldn't access her thoughts anymore.

She reached across the table and took both my hands in both of hers. They were tiny, with gnarled knuckles and large rings, but her grip was firm and warm. "Close your eyes. Think deeply," she instructed.

I closed my eyes. Opened them again. Her eyes were closed, her lips quietly chanting something I couldn't hear. I felt uncomfortable doing this. I didn't know how to meditate. I breathed deeply. Tried to relax.

And almost immediately had a vision.

The room whirled around, faster and faster, reminding me of the time when I was a kid and I would twirl around and around to make myself dizzy. When the room came to a stop, I found myself no longer holding hands with Lady Azura. I was standing in the kitchen. It seemed to be late. Very late at night. I could see snow coming down outside the window. It was heaped on the windowsill. The calendar on the wall showed that it was February of this year—just last month.

The white-haired woman from my dream stood in a corner of the kitchen, facing Lady Azura. But now the woman was no longer alive. She was clearly a spirit. She looked much older than she had in my dream. Now she was an old woman, although probably not quite as old as Lady Azura. But she looked wearier. Careworn. Her eyes darted from side to side. Her movements seemed twitchy. Nervous.

"Please. You must help me," she said to Lady Azura. Her voice was dry and cracked. Not the firm voice from my dream. Her former confidence seemed to have vanished.

Lady Azura was dressed in her dressing gown, wearing no makeup. As though she'd come into the kitchen late at night, after everyone else was in bed. Which made sense. I often thought I heard her roaming around the downstairs while I lay in bed.

Lady Azura's hands clutched the countertop behind her. I noticed her knuckles turned lighter. "I tried to help you when you were alive," she said, firmly but not unkindly. "It will be much harder now. Yet there is still a way to reverse the course. You know what you must do, Nina." My great-grandmother's brown eyes were sad. Filled with pity.

"I—cannot do it on my own," said Nina the spirit, her voice trembling.

Lady Azura looked down at the floor and sighed heavily. "I will try to help you now, but you must *help* me help you. It will be very difficult for me. I must know that you will do the right thing."

"I will. I swear," said the spirit.

Suddenly the vision shifted.

Lady Azura and the white-haired woman—still a spirit—were seated across from each other at Lady Azura's table. My great-grandmother was still wearing her dressing gown. Now I could see the clock over the entry door, and it read 1:20 a.m. I stood nearby, looking down at them, but neither seemed to know that I was there. And yet I could smell the faint scent of patchouli, hear the knocking of the old radiators, feel the chilly draft that escaped from beneath the heavy drapes at the window. Outside, icy snow pattered against the window.

Several large, green crystals lay between them. Moldavite crystals. Like the one Lady Azura had given to me.

The spirit was trembling. She looked as though she might cry. The air in the room felt dark. Heavy. I found it hard to breathe. I felt an overwhelming sense of gloom and desolation. Hopelessness.

"You must let go. You must forgive them. Tell them how you feel. Show them. Release the energy, Nina. Release it, please."

"I cannot," she gasped. "It's too late."

"You can. You must. Together we must try."

The spirit was quiet for maybe a full minute, although it was hard to know how much time was passing. Then all at once she gave a shriek. I jumped. Lady Azura's eyes flew open.

I watched as a dark cloud whooshed out of the spirit's body. It startled me so much that I gasped and jumped backward. It formed a smoky, roiling cloud, dark as a smoke cloud, but somehow even thicker.

Just like the cloud I'd seen in my room.

It occurred to me that the cloud seemed to be propelled by anger. Agitation. It whipped furiously around the room. The spirit and I followed its path, this way and that. Lady Azura sat calmly, staring at the spirit. I was certain she couldn't see the cloud. Didn't know it was there.

Then the cloud slammed into a mirror on the wall, cracking it so that long, branchlike strands grew across it, like the surface of thin ice on a pond. But it didn't make a sound. Lady Azura did not seem to notice this, either, although the spirit and I both saw it. *So that's what happened to the mirror,* I thought, remembering how the mirror had just disappeared from Lady Azura's wall one day last month, and she'd refused to tell me anything other than that it had broken.

I saw the cloud swirl and shift, and then it seemed to get sucked out of the room, under the closed door. Out into the house. Just as it had in my bedroom after my dream.

The vision ended.

"Sara? Are you all right?"

I blinked. Stared at her. I had beads of sweat on my forehead and on my upper lip. I was breathing heavily. The vision had been so . . . vivid.

Lady Azura was giving me one of her laser stares. Her eyes bore into me.

"Sara. You must tell me what happened."

Now I was officially freaked out. I'd dreamed about this woman twice. Then I'd seen her in a vision. Lady Azura clearly knew her. Suddenly I felt angry. She knew more than she was telling me. All this talk of "bad energy." I had seen with my own eyes that the bad energy had been released into our house by this spirit. It hadn't just spontaneously shown up. There was more to the story. It didn't seem right that she was holding back information from me.

I decided to just come right out with it.

"Who is Nina Oliver?"

Lady Azura went pale.

Chapter 9

When someone who wears that much makeup loses all the color from her face, you know you're onto something.

Then she recovered. She folded her hands and leaned toward me, speaking in a calm, clear voice. "Sara. It is very important that you tell me what just happened to you. Did you have a vision?"

I met her eyes. I could be just as strong. I would tell her, but first she had to tell me what she knew.

"I think you're keeping something from me," I said. "I'm not a kid. Well, I mean, I am, but I'm also old enough to handle this. You have to please tell me who Nina Oliver is. Because I have seen her three times."

She sat back. She looked surprised. I guess I'd

never really shown that I had much backbone before. I think I might have been as surprised as she was, but I tried not to show it. I just sat there and didn't look away.

"Very well. If you have seen that dreadful woman so many times, then you have a right to know." Lady Azura's eyes searched my face as she spoke. "I will tell you the story of Nina Oliver." And with that, she cleared her throat and launched into her story.

"Nina came to visit me many years ago—it was more than twenty years ago, in fact. But she came not as a client, she told me, but as a colleague. She told me that she had a special power. She was able to read people's minds."

Lady Azura sat back and regarded me. I nodded, like that information came as no surprise. I mean, I'd seen and heard firsthand the way she read my *own* mind.

Of course, I could see that Lady Azura registered my response. She continued.

"It started happening to her very suddenly, when she was in her late forties. Her children had grown. She was an attorney at a large law firm, well respected for her keen analytic mind, but, I gathered, not on a partnership track because she was not well liked by her colleagues. I could see why. She was argumentative. Unwilling to listen to what others had to say. Arrogant.

"She came to me, she said, for advice. Her powers came and went sporadically. She wanted to learn to better harness the power, so she could use it to her benefit. But she did not like what I had to say to her. I told her this power was not the gift she believed it to be, but a terrible burden, and a destructive one. I told her I would help her to rid herself of this power, if she so chose."

Now the second dream I'd had made sense. The one where Nina had given the crystal back. The one where Lady Azura had been urging her—pleading with her, really—to relinquish her power rather than to strengthen it. "So you mean, being able to read minds is always a bad thing?" I asked without meeting her eye.

"Our thoughts belong to us, Sara. They are precious. And they should be private. The choice to share our thoughts and feelings should be our own. And the ability to hear others' thoughts can be terribly destruc-tive to the one who possesses the power. But then," she said, looking at me keenly, forcing me to meet her eyes, "I suspect that you have learned this firsthand."

My breath caught in my throat. How did she know?

She continued. "At first Nina seemed to want to work with me. She came back twice. She used the moldavite crystal I gave her to work on blocking out the power. But it seems the power was too seductive. Her ability to read others' thoughts turned out to be extremely beneficial in her capacity as a litigation attorney."

"As a—what?"

"A lawyer who argues cases in court. She became a much-feared litigator who, of course, could always know what the opposition was going to do before they did it."

I nodded. I could see why reading minds would be an advantage to a lawyer.

"She came back to me one more time. But it was to return the crystal I had given to her. She told me she was working on strengthening her powers, not block-ing them. When I tried to tell her I thought she was making a huge mistake, she accused me of being jealous." Lady Azura sniffed, as though the memory was something she'd prefer not to dwell on. "She called me a charlatan."

"A what?"

"A fake. I suppose I lost my temper with her. She was not an easy person to deal with, and it was difficult to maintain one's professional composure when she turned combative. But that was the last straw. I threw her out."

"Oh," I said, suppressing a smile. I remembered my dream where my tiny great-grandmother had thrown the woman out. Leave it to Lady Azura to stand up to one of the toughest cross-examiners in the business, without so much as batting a fake eyelash.

"That was the last I saw of her for a very long time. She was promoted to partner, and then left the local firm to join a famous, high-powered corporate law firm in New York. I began reading about her cases in the newspaper. Some of them made national headlines. But she remained a deeply insecure and unhappy person at heart. She grew ever more greedy and became obsessed with her power. I heard through the grapevine that her personal life suffered greatly. She refused to do the hard work necessary to repair her broken relationships. Her husband left her. Her grown children moved far away from her. It became a vicious cycle: the more difficult she became as a person, the more frequently she read others' minds and heard their negative thoughts about her. She alienated her children's spouses. She was too critical of the way they raised her grandchildren."

"So," I said, "she was really successful professionally, but lost all her friends personally."

"That's correct." Another meaningful look my way. "She became very rich, I heard. She won the vast majority of her cases, and she defended some powerful but, shall we say, unsavory clients."

She was quiet for a time, lost in thought.

"And then what happened?" I prompted her.

"I stopped reading news of her about ten years ago. Her name had been in the papers frequently, and then suddenly it wasn't. I forgot about her, to be honest. And then, several weeks ago, she reappeared. But she was no longer a living person."

"She was a spirit," I said.

Lady Azura nodded.

I wasn't surprised by this information, of course. I'd seen her as a spirit in my vision.

"She died lonely and bitter. Her husband had remarried. Her children had stopped speaking to her. For the first time since I had known her, she appeared humble. Contrite. Alas, too late. But she told me what had happened. The last few years prior to her death, her power had reached such strength that she was unable to filter out others' thoughts at all. Everywhere she went, she heard the thoughts of the people around her. It slowly began to drive away her reason."

"You mean, she went crazy?"

"That's a harsh way to describe it, but accurate, I suppose. She quit her job. Her children helped her find a retirement community that sounds like it might have been more of a very well-financed psychiatric residency program."

I gulped.

"Her spirit told me that while there, she withdrew from the company of others more and more. She simply couldn't block out their thoughts. Eventually she fell ill and died. But death brought her no relief.

Her spirit was stuck here, and bore the same burden."

"Her spirit could also read minds?"

"Yes, and so she visited me late one night a few weeks ago, in February. I wasn't sure whether I could help her. But she was so remorseful. She begged me to help her. I pitied her. I tried to help her.

"I explained to her how spirits can become trapped here sometimes. I told her that we had to exorcise the negative energy from within her spirit. She had to start by forgiving herself, and more importantly, others. She had to acknowledge that people are flawed—not just herself, but all the people who had once loved her. That everyone harbors thoughts deep inside that are just that: thoughts. Practically everyone has dark thoughts, but these thoughts are not meant to be overheard. They're a way by which people work through issues in the safety of their minds."

I had the feeling that she was talking as much about me as she was about Nina Oliver.

"Nina had never understood her power while she was alive. I felt she had to reach that step before she would be able to move on. So we had a session, such as I have never had before with someone who has passed on to the spirit world. Highly unusual. And very difficult for me. I am still not sure of the outcome of that session."

"So that's what I saw," I murmured as it all became clear to me.

Lady Azura looked at me sharply. "What did you see?"

"The vision I had just now. It was of your session together. Of you trying to help her."

Lady Azura sat up even straighter in her chair. "Sara, this is extremely important. I need you to tell me exactly what you saw."

So I told her what I had seen. About the black cloud. About the broken mirror. About how the cloud vanished underneath the door.

When she heard about the way the black cloud had escaped from the spirit and broken the mirror, she drew in a sharp breath. Like that explained a lot.

Then I told her everything else. About my dreams. About the black cloud over my bed. And about my own ability to read minds. How it seemed to be gaining in strength and frequency with every passing day.

Lady Azura listened intently. "This explains so

much," she said when I was finished. "I have not seen Nina's spirit since that night, several weeks ago. I did not see the cloud you speak of, but I discovered the cracked mirror after she had gone. I was not sure how the two things were related, but I knew they were somehow.

"It makes a great deal of sense that her negative energy was released from her spirit and into this house. I began to suspect your newfound ability to read minds soon after that happened. Now my suspicions are confirmed."

"So Nina's powers transferred from her to me?"

"It seems so. Whether it was that Nina's energy somehow attached to your aura, or whether it simply triggered something that was a latent power you already possessed, remains to be seen."

"Lady Azura, I don't want this power. I don't want to turn out like Nina. Can you help me?" I begged.

She clasped my hands. "Of course I can help you, Sara. You are going to have to follow what I say and work very hard, but if you want to, we can get rid of this power together."

Chapter 10

I heard the determination in Lady Azura's voice, but I was worried. What if I *couldn't* get rid of this power? Would I end up like Nina? Driving everyone I loved away from me? Landing in the loony bin?

Lady Azura seemed to be able to read my thoughts. She patted my hand. "Nina was weak and fell victim to her powers. But you, Sara, are strong. Much stronger than she. Perhaps stronger than I." Her brown eyes twinkled. "This negative energy has been swirling around the house for a while now. It has latched on to you. It is not like your other powers."

Now that she had gotten to the bottom of what was happening in the house, Lady Azura seemed reinvigorated. She strode around her room, opening drawers and cabinets, gathering crystals and bringing them to the table.

"I know. I hate it," I said as my eyes followed her around the room. "I think it's made me depressed or something. I've been moping around all week, feeling sorry for myself because no one cares that my birthday is coming up. And because I've been reading my friends' minds. And every time I do, I feel bad about what I hear."

"Together we will help you learn to block the ability," she said. "It may be difficult at first, but the more you do it, the easier it will become for you." She spoke with such conviction that I started to believe we could really do this.

"You mean it's like riding a bike or learning to whistle?"

"Exactly."

Haltingly, I told her how I had been able to block it out a few times on my own by imagining I was putting a bubble up around me.

"Sara, that is wonderful news," Lady Azura exclaimed as her face lit up. "That was your own instincts, guiding you in the right direction." The worried look on her face was now completely gone. She blinked her eyes rapidly as she spoke to me. "Let's use this bubble you talk about; it is your shield. Visualize it now. But instead of using it defensively, to block out others and fend off their thoughts, use it as a positive energy force. Try now," she urged.

So I tried to conjure up the bubble. I closed my eyes. Thought positive thoughts. Opened my eyes. I could see the bubble shimmering and silvery all around me, like I was inside some freaky spacecraft.

"I did it!" I shouted, springing up. "Can you see it? Can you see the bubble?"

She smiled and shook her head. "I cannot see it. But you have astonishing powers, Sara. And unlike Nina, you are able not only to block this negative energy, but to produce a positive force to change its very nature. You did not bring this on yourself, nor did you invite it, so it will be far easier for you to offset it."

We spent the next two hours practicing. It was one of the most exhausting things I had ever done. It was so hard at first. I couldn't produce the bubble quite so easily the next few times I tried. At first it was like a weak force field. I could actually watch as Lady Azura's thoughts bounced against it, but then it would drop like a popped soap bubble, and I would be able to hear her thoughts rushing in. I could hear her worrying about me. Worrying about my father and his fears about the house. I suspected that she was letting me hear her thoughts. On purpose. That she was able to let me hear them, or not, at will.

I tried harder.

And gradually I got better at it.

By now it was evening. It was almost time for dinner, I realized, but I wasn't even hungry. I felt drained, but happy, too. I jumped up from my chair. "Can I go practice?" I asked her. "I want to go find Lily. Or some of my other friends, and see if I can block them."

She nodded. "Go ahead, my dear. Go and be strong."

I raced out the door and down the sidewalk toward Lily's house.

Just as I skidded to a stop at her front walkway, I saw her emerging from the door with Miranda, Avery, and Marlee.

"Sara!" yelled Lily. She looked happy to see me. But

was she really? I started to tune in to her thoughts. It would be so easy to do. So tempting to listen in. I'd discovered the hard way that kids my age so often said one thing and thought another. I could feel the temptation start to win.

Then I stopped myself. I didn't want to end up like Nina. Closing my eyes, I conjured up the bubble.

It worked. Lily's thoughts bounced off my bubble. I refused to hear them. Maybe she was glad to see me, and maybe she wasn't.

"Hey, guys!" I said, swallowing my hurt feelings. So what if they were all hanging out together? Without me. Maybe it was a school thing or something.

"We were just hanging out!" said Lily as the three of them joined me. "And we were about to walk over to your house to see if you were around. I know you were in a hurry to get home, so I figured you had to help out your great-grandmother. And now here you are!"

I chose to believe her. I chose not to think that they so were not on their way to see me, and that she made up the story so my feelings wouldn't be hurt. I chose not to let down my bubble and read their thoughts to see what they really were thinking. I chose, as my dad might put it, to give them the benefit of the doubt.

And ended up having a really fun time.

The early evening air was cool and smelled of damp earth and sea air. We decided to walk down to the beach. I love the beach when no one else is there. We found an old Frisbee half-buried in the sand and spent the next half hour tossing it, collecting shells, just having fun. I kept wishing I'd brought my camera with me. And then it was time to get home for dinner.

When I got home, my father was already in the kitchen. He still seemed stressed out. Grim-faced. He was breading chicken breasts and boiling water for potatoes. I helped by making a salad with my own homemade vinaigrette that Mrs. Randazzo had taught me how to make. My dad usually loved that dressing, and I secretly hoped it would cheer him up. But he remained pretty quiet as he prepared dinner.

As soon as I had the chance, I escaped from dinner prepping and went to find Lady Azura. She was in her room, sitting in her old padded rocking chair, watching the news and shaking her head in dismay at what was going on in the world.

I told her about the success I'd had with my friends. She seemed pleased.

"I'm worried, though," I said. "My dad still seems really stressed. About money. About the house. Not that I read his thoughts or anything," I added quickly.

"You've done well today, Sara. Now you must continue to think positive thoughts," said Lady Azura. "I believe your father is just worried about you and your safety. I don't think he will take any drastic steps anytime soon. Continue as you did today. Block out thoughts and embrace the good. Together we will eventually rid the house of this negative energy."

"But isn't there *more* that we can do?" I asked. "It all feels so . . . defensive, rather than offensive. We keep trying to block, to fend off, to think away the bad stuff. I feel like we ought to be able to take charge, chase it away. Can't we, like, summon Nina and get her to take back the energy she left here?"

But Lady Azura shook her head, clearly unwilling to consider what I was suggesting. "Sara, that is unnecessary. We needn't meddle with this negative energy more than we absolutely have to. It will be enough to believe in your power to think positively. It might not be the fastest solution, but it will work eventually. We will reclaim our house!"

"But I'm scared to go to sleep. What if I have more bad dreams? What if I wake up in that awful dark cloud again?"

Lady Azura smiled. "You must do what you do naturally. Tap into your capacity to love. Count your blessings. Before you fall asleep, think about the people in life that you love the most dearly. That is the best way to drive away the negative energy. I do that every night, whether my house is under attack by dark energy or not."

I nodded. Thanked her and left. But I wasn't convinced.

"I may need some help fixing the garage," my dad said to us over dinner. "Some of the wall that came down revealed some real structural damage. We'll need to fix it if we want to improve the resale value of this place. And the truck is going to need quite a bit of bodywork. Vern sent me to a good guy over in Ocean Heights who is going to work on it for me, but it's going to be expensive."

Lady Azura and I both nodded. Then we all kept eating. The only sound was the scrape of forks on plates for a while. I resisted the strong urge to read my dad's mind. I felt that if I did, I would be scared by what I heard. I just knew he was thinking about how dangerous he thought this house was. He was worried about me. And even about Lady Azura. I hadn't liked the sound of the phrase "resale value." Was he really thinking about convincing Lady Azura to sell the house? I pushed the unsettling thought away.

I knew it was up to me to change the energy in the house. To change my father's mind. I needed to do something beyond what Lady Azura advised. Something more powerful than just thinking happy thoughts. I needed to root out the problem, like a weed. To stop the negative energy from doing more damage.

An idea began to form in my mind.

Later that night I was in bed, finishing my English reading, when my dad poked his head into my room.

"Got a sec, kiddo?"

"I suppose I can tear myself away from *The Odyssey*

for a second," I said with a grin, putting down my book.

He sat down at the edge of my bed. He looked more tired than usual, but still handsome, in a crinkly-eyed, rumpled-hair, needs-a-shave kind of way.

"Listen, kiddo, I hope you were okay with our doing something special for your birthday on a different day," he said. "I know you have that party to go to on Saturday, and it's kind of a crazy weekend for me, work-wise. And now I don't have a car, either. The body shop says it won't be ready until at least Thursday, and much as I love driving Lady Azura's boat"—he rolled his eyes—"I don't want to drive it any kind of distance. So maybe we can plan a getaway for, say, *next* weekend? I was thinking—"

"Dad," I interrupted. "No worries. I totally understand." And I did. The last thing I wanted was for him to be feeling bad about my birthday, on top of all the other stuff he was worrying about. "I really wasn't upset about not doing something together," I continued. "I was more upset because Lily's being kind of, I don't know, weird and standoffish about this party she's having. And it's a party for Jayden. You know, the guy I went to the semiformal dance with a few weeks ago. And she pretty much forgot all about the fact that it was the same day as my birthday. But I think she feels bad about forgetting."

He opened his mouth as though he wanted to say something, then closed it again. I had a sudden urge to read his thoughts, but again I resisted. I put up the bubble. This time it was easy. And then I was glad I wasn't intruding into his personal thoughts.

"I know friend stuff can be tough," he said awkwardly. "But you just have to trust that you and Lily are really good friends. And not worry too much about the small stuff. Just think positive, kiddo."

I smiled. All this talk about positive thinking! But I knew he was trying. I knew he worried all the time that I didn't have a mother around to say these kinds of motherly things. They sounded a little awkward coming from my dad, but it made me love him all the more for trying. "Thanks, Daddy-o," I said, using my old nickname for him. That made him smile.

He patted my leg and stood up. "Try to get some sleep."

I dropped my book onto the floor next to my bed

and snuggled into my pillows. He kissed me on the forehead and turned out the light.

But I didn't fall asleep. As soon as I was sure I heard him walk down the hall and into his room, I turned my light back on and sat up. I had my own plan of how to fix the problems in my house, and I was going to try it tonight.

Chapter 11

I finished my *Odyssey* reading and even got ahead in my social studies chapter before I decided that everyone else in the house must be asleep. Usually reading one page of my social studies textbook was enough to put me to sleep, but not tonight. I was wide-awake. Apprehensive, but excited, too. The clock said 12:04 a.m. What I planned to do was risky, because Lady Azura was a night owl. But she'd yawned through dinner and grumbled several times about turning in early. So I had to hope for the best.

I didn't dare go downstairs to Lady Azura's summoning room. Even if she had gone to bed, I couldn't risk it. She was a light sleeper and would probably hear me.

I swung my legs out of bed and tiptoed over to my

bureau, where I'd hid the candle I had borrowed from Lady Azura's room earlier in the evening. I carried it over to my desk, which I'd decluttered in anticipation of this occasion. I lit the candle and then sat down, staring into the flame.

I didn't know how to summon a spirit properly, but I'd done it once before with Jayden's brother, Marco, and I felt pretty sure I could do it again.

"Nina Oliver," I whispered, closing my eyes. "Nina, if you can hear me, please show yourself. I—I am Sara Collins. I want to help you. Please?"

I opened my eyes. Nothing. My room was the same old room. Cluttered bureau. Lots of clothes all over the floor. Books and photography stuff strewn around near my reading chair in the corner. I was a naturally untidy person, and my dad wasn't big on reminding me to clean my room. Whatever. I sighed. This wasn't working.

A cloud must have finished passing over the moon, because my room filled with silver light. I could see the picture of my mother next to my bed from where I sat. I looked over at it, trying to gain strength and resolve. I clutched the moldavite crystal

Lady Azura had given me. I tried again.

"Nina Oliver? I was hoping you could just, um, drop by for a chat? I know this is a little unconventional, me summoning you up here and all. But please. Could you show yourself?"

I opened my eyes. Still nothing.

Wait.

There was something.

The candle flickered. Went out.

And then lit again.

My foot began tingling. My breathing grew shallow. A silver shimmer that I thought was the mirror turned out to be behind me, reflected in the mirror in front of me. I turned around slowly. A spirit was beginning to materialize.

I realized I'd been holding my breath, and I let it out quickly, shakily. My heart thudded in my chest.

Nina Oliver was now a solid-looking form, faintly glowing in the dim light from the moon. She strode across the room and stood in front of me. Hastily, I stood up to meet her.

"Well? What do you want?" she demanded.

It was the same woman. The woman from my

dreams. Long white hair, down to the shoulders. A business suit and sensible shoes. If you looked at her quickly, and didn't know she was a spirit, you might mistake her for a lawyer or a banker. But if you really paid attention, you would notice something wrong. Something off about the expression on her face. Her eyes. They kept darting from side to side, then down to the floor, not meeting my gaze. She looked annoyed, like I'd interrupted her in the middle of an important business call.

Out of the corner of my eye, I became aware of a swirling movement. It was the dark cloud. It seemed to grow larger and larger, billowing around the room. Then it swirled around the two of us. It seemed to engulf us, so I could only see her as though through a gauzy haze. I felt cold all of a sudden. The hopeless feeling returned. What was I doing? Why was I even attempting this? This spirit wasn't going to change. She wasn't going to help me. She was mean and hateful even in death. The way she was in life.

I tried to control my thoughts. *Don't lose hope. Don't judge. Don't think anything critical. She had a hard time when she was alive. Maybe on some level she really wants my help. Try. Don't give up.*

"Oh, so that's what you think, is it?" she practically spat at me. "You think I want your help? That I am to be pitied?"

She can hear my thoughts.

"Of course I can hear your thoughts! Don't you realize how powerful this ability made me in life? No one could stop me. No one was invulnerable."

I tried to conjure up the bubble. The one that I'd been practicing, which blocked me from hearing other people's thoughts. Maybe it could help block *my* thoughts from reaching her.

"It's no use. You cannot block me."

The bubble failed. A wave of nausea clenched my stomach, and I suddenly felt dizzy. I clutched the edge of my desk. I had to do something. It was an awful feeling, knowing my thoughts were swirling from my head into hers. Now I understood how other people must feel. Maybe they didn't know that I was hearing their thoughts. But maybe at some subconscious level, they did.

"Please. Stop," I said out loud.

She laughed, but not in a nice way.

I had to struggle to stay calm. Not to cry. Not to get angry.

"Don't fight this power," she said. "You, too, can grow stronger. Smarter. Better than everyone around you. Why do you not see it as a gift? Something only you and I and very few others share?"

Positive. Think positive thoughts. I closed my eyes. Conjured up the image of my mother in my mind.

"She cannot help you!"

Conjured up my father's crinkly-eyed smile.

"Nor can he! He is not like us. He distrusts your powers. He's constantly worrying about you. People who worry, who fret, do not advance in life. They do not climb high. You are different."

I conjured up Lady Azura's wise, bright face. Skin like crepe paper, but eyes that were still full of life. Intelligence. Wit. Love. Love for me.

"Ha! She tried to thwart me every moment. She is not someone you should turn to at a time like this. Listen to me, Sara. . . ."

The dark cloud continued to swirl around us. I felt isolated. As though she and I were the only two beings in a vast wasteland. And she was a spirit. I kept concentrating. Positive thoughts.

"But you came to her. To Lady Azura. You asked her to help you. To rid yourself of the bad energy. You haven't changed. You must still wish for this," I said.

"I had a moment of weakness. I took the power back."

I pushed the negative thoughts—the fear, the anxiety, the worry—from my mind. She *had* tried to get rid of the power. I'd seen her do it with Lady Azura. I'd seen the cloud leave her and get released into the house. Maybe she didn't mean what she was saying right now. Maybe it was the cloud that was controlling her now. Controlling me.

Had I made a terrible mistake in bringing her back here? Had I made the negative energy reattach itself to this spirit? I had to be strong for both of us. For me and for the spirit. Lady Azura had told me I was strong. Now I had to prove it.

I thought of my love for my family. For my mother. I reached deep and put myself in Nina's place. I felt sympathy for her, for the sad life she must have led. I felt forgiveness.

The dark cloud began to swirl faster. Around and around us.

Then it started to break up. Interspersed with the black cloud, I started to see white, silvery light. That lighter cloud was back. And it was fighting the dark cloud. Had I made it appear?

Now I could see the objects in my room. The darkness was becoming sparkly. Silvery. Lighter.

I thought harder. Clutched my crystal. Watched the cloud lighten.

"What are you doing?" gasped the spirit.

"Nina," I said, in a pleading tone. "You must let go. Really. This ability to read people's thoughts? It's not a good thing. I'm trying to fight it. You can too."

"Stop," she said, but her voice was now trembly, wobbly, weaker. The firm, angry tone was gone.

I grew more confident. "I liked the power I had to read minds too. At first. But then I realized it just made me feel bad. It made me upset with people I love. It's really not a good thing. I figured out how to put up this block thing, so their thoughts couldn't get through. Couldn't get into my own mind."

The spirit began to weep. Her ghostly hands flew to her face, her shoulders hunched up, and she began shaking, her body racked with sobs.

I stood there awkwardly. Should I say something? Apologize? Try to pat her on the shoulder? I decided the best thing to do was to just stand there, quietly, and wait for her to say something.

Soon she did.

She pulled her hands away from her face and regarded me silently, no longer sobbing. But her face was all twisted up with sadness.

The black cloud appeared to be gone.

"I drove away my family," she whispered. Her voice was suddenly much weaker, much softer. I wasn't sure whether she was talking to me or to herself. "I behaved very, very badly. I told my daughter, Dolores, her husband was a fool. That he had huge second thoughts about marriage. That he still loved his old girlfriend."

I cringed. I wasn't a grown-up, of course, but even a twelve-year-old kid can tell those are not thoughts that should be revealed.

"I told my son, Sebastian, that his new wife was shallow. That she wasn't his intellectual equal. That he would grow tired of being married to such a dimwit. He grew very angry at me. But I heard her thoughts! I heard her vacuous, empty, shallow thoughts!"

I gulped. How many times had I had vacuous, empty, shallow thoughts myself? Didn't everyone day-dream from time to time? Think about dumb stuff? I didn't say anything. She looked upset enough already.

"And Harold. He told me I drove him crazy, know-ing what he was thinking all the time. He said he felt like he was in one of those dreams, where you show up for work without any clothes on. He felt exposed. Vulnerable. Frightened to think anything. He left me."

New sobs.

I wished Lady Azura were there. She'd know what to say. She always knew what to say. All I could do was just stand there awkwardly, first on one foot, then the other. Scratching the back of my calf with my big toe. Then the other calf with the other big toe. Finally she stopped crying. Again.

"What should I do? Tell me how to make it better." She was now staring at me, appealing to me. Like I knew?

I took a step back. Me? How would *I* know what to do? I thought about asking her to wait. To stay right there, while I ran downstairs to wake up Lady Azura and ask her what to say. But I couldn't. Lady Azura had told me she hadn't been upstairs in years. And anyway, she'd probably be furious with me for conjuring a spirit without her knowledge. And who was to say the spirit would be willing to hang around, waiting for me to return? No. I had to think of something to say all by myself.

"Well," I began, trying to stall for time. My mind was rapidly calculating. I began again. More confidently. "You should go visit them. Your family. Even if they can't see you. You can send them positive thoughts. Loving thoughts. Ask them to forgive you. Tell them *you* understand why they turned their backs on you. Tell them that you still love them."

Suddenly she looked like a small child. "Do you think that would work? Really?"

I had no idea if it would work. But I nodded confidently.

She smiled at me. She looked different now. Nicer. Less angry. More willing to listen.

"Thank you," she said.

Before I could say anything, she vanished.

Chapter 12

I blew out the candle. The room was still light, from the moon outside or from the silvery cloud inside, I wasn't sure. I saw no sign of the dark cloud anywhere. And I felt better. Happier. More upbeat in practically every way.

I glanced at my mother's picture as I climbed back into bed. I think I fell asleep with a smile on my face.

And woke up a few hours later, wide awake.

I glanced at the clock. It read 3:33. My room seemed brightly lit. As my eyes adjusted to being open and awake, I realized that I was enveloped in the silvery cloud. My mind felt peaceful. Happy.

I sat up. *This must be what positive energy feels like,* I thought. As I watched, the silvery cloud began to move. It swirled around my bedroom, illuminating objects one by one. It reminded me of the time my dad had taken me to the circus, and there had been a spotlight that beamed and swept the crowd, the rings, the performers. I felt giddy with happiness—the opposite of the way I'd felt about the dark cloud, which had made me feel scared. Anxious. Upset.

The cloud swirled beneath my door and vanished. I practically leaped out of bed, borderline skipped to the door. Pulled it open and followed the silvery light.

I saw it swirl into my dad's bedroom. His door was open. I tiptoed down the hall, avoiding the familiar places on the floor that I knew would squeak if stepped on. I glanced into his room.

He was sleeping. And I could see his dream. Was that wrong? Should I have put up the bubble? Somehow it didn't feel wrong. Just for a minute. He was dreaming about my mother. I could see her. The two were having a picnic on the beach. They looked young. Happy. I could smell the salty air. Hear the roar of the surf. The cawing of seagulls in the distance.

That was enough. I didn't need to stay. It was enough to know that my dad was dreaming a happy dream.

The cloud whooshed toward me and enveloped me in the doorway of my dad's room for a moment. During that short second or two, I felt a wave of— what did Lady Azura call it one time?—euphoria. That's what it was. And then it was past me, and swirling down the hall. I had the distinct feeling it wanted me to follow. So I did.

I tiptoed as quietly as I could down the creaky front-hall stairs and into the shadowy front hallway. I saw the cloud swirl into the kitchen. I followed it. I was just in time to see it vanish under Lady Azura's door.

Laughing lightly to myself, I stole across the kitchen and opened the door that led to her room. I tiptoed down the short hallway and glanced into her room.

She was sleeping peacefully. Her hair was tucked up into a frilly white cap. I had no idea people still wore such things. Her thin arms were outside the covers, and her hands were clasped serenely across her stomach. She looked like she was dreaming. A happy dream.

And then I saw her dream.

Her daughter, Diana, just a few years older than

me. That was my grandmother. And Lady Azura's husband, Richard. My great-grandfather. The three were sitting at the dinner table in the kitchen. The kitchen looked almost the same. Different curtains. Different coffeemaker. An old-fashioned stand mixer on the counter. But the table was the same. The color was the same. I stared at my grandmother-to-be. The three of them were laughing and chatting. Lady Azura looked so young!

That was enough. I didn't want to intrude any further. I turned away from her room, out of the kitchen, and back upstairs. I fell into bed and sank into a dreamless sleep.

When I opened my eyes a few hours later, the clock read 6:37. But I felt awake. Refreshed. Maybe it was a day-before-my-birthday sort of feeling. Or maybe I felt this way because I'd succeeded in ridding the house of negative energy. And filling it with positive.

Whatever the reason, I was humming to myself as I walked into the kitchen ten minutes later. Lady Azura was still sleeping. That was a good sign. Maybe she hadn't had any more bad dreams to keep her awake.

My dad wasn't there either. He'd left for work early, in Lady Azura's huge light-blue car.

I hummed my way through breakfast.

Lily was waiting for me when I reached her house.

"Hey!" I said. "How is the party planning going?"

She made a face. "Fine. A pain. But fine."

"Need any, um, help?"

"I think I'm good. Miranda and I are going shopping together this afternoon."

I nodded, staring at the ground as we walked. I felt no urge to read her thoughts, but my feelings were definitely still hurt. Hadn't she said she was going to visit her aunt this afternoon? And didn't I know, from having read her thoughts before, that she and Miranda were going to shop for a present for Jayden together? I knew I should talk to her about it. But while I was trying to figure out a way to bring it up, we were joined by Jayden.

"Hey!" he said, falling into step with us.

"Where'd you come from?" asked Lily cheerfully. "I thought you took the bus to school."

"Usually I do," he said, "but my mom is on a mission right now. Heading to the home store for boxes and stuff. And I saw you guys walking, so I had her drop me off to walk the rest of the way with you."

I was pretty sure I had the usual dopey grin on my face that I always got when I was near Jayden. He had that effect on me. A combination of making me feel totally foolish and totally comfortable when I was in his presence. I darted a glance at him. Something about that lanky, athletic stride. That dark, wavy hair. It was tragic that he was going to be moving away. But then, we were only twelve. What was the guy's name we'd studied in English class last semester? Alfred, Lord Someone. As Alfred put it, "'Tis better to have loved and lost, than never to have loved at all."

Now I was sure I'd banished the negative energy. A few days ago I had been unable to even think about Jayden leaving, because it made me feel too confused and upset. And now . . . well, I still felt sad, but it wasn't the same. I felt at peace with it.

"So are you still planning on coming to the party tomorrow night, or did you get a better offer?" Jayden asked, nudging me with his elbow playfully.

"Yeah, I thought I'd put in an appearance," I said with a little shrug. "I had to turn down five other invitations, but that's fine. Whatever."

"Thanks. I'm so honored," he said.

We heard the first bell ring as we approached the front steps of the school.

"Oops. Gotta run," he said, breaking into a trot. "Forgot my grammar workbook and have to do it before the second bell rings!"

"Good luck with that!" I shouted to his departing figure.

Lily and I headed into school with the rest of the kids.

"I wonder if he even knows it's my birthday," I said, more to myself than to Lily, as we made our way to our lockers through the crowded hallway.

Lily turned to me, stunned. "Wow. Never even occurred to me to tell him. I just assumed he'd know. But then, if *you* haven't told him, how *would* he know?"

"Well, I might have mentioned it a long time ago," I said. "But don't tell him, okay?" We were at our lockers. "He'd just feel bad that he forgot, and I want this party to be about him, not me."

"Good point," said Lily.

"But it did occur to me . . . ," I said as we hustled

to class. "I don't have a going-away present for him. I guess I should get one."

"Oh! Yeah, you might want to get on that," said Lily.

"Gee, thanks!" I called after her as she raced away to her first class.

As I sank into my chair in class, I thought again about how Lily and Miranda were going shopping this afternoon. For *Jayden*. And hadn't invited me. I sighed. I was determined not to let Lily's new-best-friend kind of friendship with Miranda bother me. Maybe it was just a phase. Because they were in the same dance class or something. But I really needed to talk to her about this.

Chapter 13

After school that day I found Lady Azura in the kitchen, having her usual cup of tea. She had put out a cup and saucer for me. I would have preferred milk and cookies, but then I realized I was almost a teenager. I should start acting more grown-up.

She poured me out a cup of steaming tea. My stomach growled. Lunch today had been dismal again. I was pretty sure they had used the leftover taco meat from the other day for the meat loaf they had served today.

"So did you sleep better last night?" I asked, tipping a lot of milk into my teacup.

"Much," she said mildly. "No bad dreams. No waking up in a mass of worries. But then, that probably does not surprise you."

She did not look up to meet my gaze. She just took a dainty sip of tea and set her cup down gently into its saucer.

"Um, that's good," I said. Did she know that I'd conjured the spirit of Nina Oliver? Was she mad at me?

"How is your work going?" she asked me.

I knew what she meant. My work with blocking out others' thoughts.

"I'm getting pretty good at it," I said. "The more I try, the easier it seems to get."

She nodded approvingly. "Your powers grow stronger and stronger. And your self-confidence as well."

What did she mean by that? Now I was worried again.

"I am glad to see you are growing and maturing into a strong-willed person," she continued. "I believe you inherited that from me," she added with a wry smile. "But like me, you appear also to have good judgment."

I was still percolating what she'd said when I heard the Boat pull into the driveway. My dad was home already! I couldn't remember a time in recent months he'd been home so early from work.

A minute later my father burst in, laden down with a huge shopping bag filled with something that smelled delicious. I jumped up to greet him and ask him what he was doing home already.

"I took off early and stopped at Thai Taste on the way home," he said as he set the shopping bag on the counter. "Figured we could have a little birthday celebration tonight, since my daughter is such a social butterfly these days and doesn't have time to spend with us on her *actual* birthday."

I knew I was smiling from ear to ear, but this was perfect. Exactly what I needed. To be celebrated by my loved ones. To eat delicious Thai food. And to forget all about friend drama, at least for a little while.

"You went all the way to Thai Taste?" I asked as I peered into the bag. Thai Taste was, hands down, the best Thai place in a twenty-five-mile radius, but there were several places much closer to our house and my dad's work. I smiled even more as I realized that he had driven miles out of the way just to go to my favorite restaurant. He shrugged like it was nothing and grinned back at me. He looked happy that I was so happy.

It was a delicious meal. Midway through, my dad finally admitted that this was quite possibly the best Thai food on the planet, and vowed to never make us eat takeout from any of the so-so Thai places nearby again. And then Lady Azura brought out a tiramisu cake from Prudente's, which is this amazing Italian bakery in town. Lily's mom always has cakes from Prudente's at their family get-togethers; I was pretty sure the Randazzos were somehow related to the Prudente family. We'd had the tiramisu cake at Lily's on Christmas Eve, and I think Lady Azura must have remembered how much I loved it. It was the perfect end to the perfect meal.

As I was scraping the last bits of gooey goodness from my plate, I saw my dad and Lady Azura exchange a look. Lady Azura stood up and went into her bedroom. She returned a minute later with a rectangular box and placed it in front of me. It looked like it might be a picture frame. People give me those a lot, I guess because I'm a photographer.

I tore away the paper and gasped. A brand-new, latest-model, computer graphics tablet, with image-editing software. The kind of thing that can edit photos and that lets you paint and draw and sketch with the electronic pen. I'd been dying for one but hadn't even dared mention it, knowing how tight money was.

"How did you—how can we—I can't believe you actually—" I couldn't finish the sentence.

"We must have read your mind," said Lady Azura drily.

My dad patted my hand. "Lady Azura and I decided to chip in together and get you something special. Is it the right kind of gizmo?"

"Yes!" I squealed. "It is *totally* the right kind of gizmo!"

My dad looked relieved. "I called Lily and asked her to help me order the right thing. She seemed pretty sure this was the right model. It's a little overwhelming for old guys like me to know what to get."

Lady Azura sniffed. "Well, I'm sure I don't know what you see in such a gizmo, but I hope you like it all the same. Now go. We'll clean up. Try it out. Show us what sort of magic that flashy-looking device can do."

I leaped from the table and gave them both a huge hug. Then I ran upstairs to my craft room to try it out.

It would be the perfect thing for making a

going-away present for Jayden. I called up a picture that we'd had taken at the semiformal a few weeks ago. Then I figured out how to use the electronic pen and spent a happy hour manipulating the photo of the two of us in a bunch of different ways, printing out the versions I liked, until I had one I was happy with. Basically the original picture, but with enhanced colors and cool special effects and a psychedelic, patterned background, which I thought was a huge improvement over the dull, fake-blue-sky backdrop that the photographer had been using. The finished product looked pretty cool.

Then I took an ordinary frame I had bought on sale and spent another half hour painting and decorating it to make it personalized just for Jayden. When the frame was dry and I put the photo into it, I was pleased with the result. I wrapped it up.

I spent the rest of the night playing with a bunch of other photos, manipulating them, enhancing them, changing the effects, drawing stuff on them. Before I knew it, my dad was knocking on the door.

"Time for bed, kiddo," he said, after he'd admired what I'd done. He stared at some of the pictures and shook his head in admiration. "Your mother would be proud. You're so much like her. So creative and talented."

I put an arm around his waist. "And what about you? Did she teach you how to take good pictures? I love the one you took of her. It's really well composed."

He gave me a sideways grin. "Believe it or not, I used to be pretty into art myself," he said. "Painting, actually. But that was a long time ago. Before marriage and baby and mortgage and—" He stopped.

I'd guessed what he was going to say without needing to read his mind. He'd been about to say, "And before I lost your mom." Or something to that effect.

I hugged him tighter.

"Why don't you try painting again?" I asked him quietly.

He looked down at me and stroked my hair. "Maybe I will sometime soon," he said. "Maybe I just might."

Chapter 14

When I woke up the next morning, I could smell the warm air. It was going to be a beautiful day. A beautiful spring birthday day that was also a Saturday. I jumped out of bed feeling happy. No matter how much I wasn't going to be celebrating, it was still my birthday.

"Hey! Back in bed!" I heard my dad's voice at the door. He was carrying a tray. Breakfast in bed. Giggling, I scrambled back under the covers and shimmied backward so I was propped up and ready for my breakfast tray.

He'd made my favorite breakfast in the world: cinnamon toast, hot cocoa, and a perfectly ripe mango, cut into cubes.

"Happy birthday, kiddo," said my dad, sitting down next to me while I took a sip of cocoa. "I can't believe my baby is a teenager! Where did the time go?"

I smiled and offered him some toast. He took a piece.

"So have you and Lily talked about your, uh, disagreement yet?" he asked.

I felt my love for my dad rise up in me. I knew he was trying to show me that he was there for me, to talk with me about my day-to-day troubles and stuff. He was so charmingly . . . awkward doing it. Not his fault. He was the same way with talking—or not—about my powers. He knew I had them but was clueless about how to advise me. That was a huge reason he'd moved us from California to live with Lady Azura. So I'd have someone to talk with about them.

"Not yet. But I will," I promised him. And I meant it.

"What do you say you and I do something special today?" my dad proposed. "Just the two of us?"

"I thought you had to fix the garage," I said.

He shrugged. "The garage can wait. It's a beautiful day. What say we drive to the aquarium? It's only a couple of towns over, and it might be fun to drive there in the Boat."

"I've been wanting to go there since I heard about

it, so that sounds great!" I said, nodding my head.

He swallowed. "I haven't been back since, since—well, it's been a long time. The last time your mother and I went there, she was pregnant with you. It was one of your mother's favorite places to go. I was trying to come up with something special for us to do today, and I thought of that." His eyes grew a little shiny.

I squeezed his hand. "That would be the perfect thing to do today, Daddy."

We spent the day at the aquarium. It was a huge place, with penguins, belugas, and an enormous fish tank that rose three stories high. You could walk around and around it on an inclined ramp that went all the way up. We watched a diver dive into the big tank to feed the fish, including several large sharks. I guess the sharks were so well fed, they weren't interested in eating the diver, but I was nervous for him just the same. Then we went to a petting area where you could pet tiny sharks and flat fish called rays that swam around in a shallow, open petting tank. Finally we walked outside and visited the bottlenose dolphins.

We got home late in the afternoon. I'd forgotten to

bring along my phone, and I found a bunch of texts from Marlee, Miranda, Avery, Tamara—all wishing me a happy birthday. And three were from Lily. She'd sent the last one just half an hour before, telling me to come to her house early so she could give me my birthday present before Jayden's party.

Since it was my birthday, I put slightly more thought than usual into my outfit, choosing a silky pink top to wear with my jeans instead of my usual T-shirt and wearing my hair down, all loose and wavy, instead of in its usual sloppy ponytail. I looked around my room, wishing I had some sort of great accessory to add to my outfit to jazz it up, but all I had was my necklace with the crystals, and that was mostly hidden under my shirt. Oh well.

An hour later I was on Lily's kitchen doorstep, carrying Jayden's wrapped picture. My mind was swirling with conflicting emotions: happiness that it was my birthday, jealousy that Miranda seemed to be Lily's new best friend, sadness that Jayden was leaving. The drama of middle school didn't suddenly change when one had a birthday, I discovered.

"Saraaaaaaaa!" yelled Lily, opening the door and

throwing her arms around me. "Happy birthday!"

She pulled me into the kitchen, which smelled of delicious things cooking. I was immediately engulfed in Randazzo warmth and chaos. Mrs. Randazzo also gave me a huge hug as Lily's brothers and little sister swirled around the place, yelling, talking, eating, singing, laughing.

"We're baking ten zillion cupcakes for Jayden's party," said Lily with a grin. "It was Mom's brilliant idea to have cupcakes, so we don't have to bother with forks and plates. Come. Help me frost this batch."

For the next hour, Lily and I frosted cupcakes, lugged bags of stuff to the car, and chatted and laughed. All my jealousy and hurt feelings evaporated. Maybe Lily made everyone feel like they were her best friend, but I was content to feel that I held that status at the moment, anyway.

"What about the decorating?" I asked as we carried the last two trays to Mrs. Randazzo's car.

"Miranda, Avery, and Marlee are handling that as we speak," said Lily. "But let's walk over to Scoops now to help them. There's no room for us in Mom's car, anyway."

"I'll text you when I'm on my way," said Mrs. Randazzo.

"Wait!" yelled Lily. "Almost forgot your birthday present!" She raced upstairs and returned a few minutes later with a small box carefully wrapped in pink paper with a silver bow on top.

"Here. From me. To you."

"Thanks, Lily," I said, suddenly feeling shy around my best friend.

"Open it!" she urged, smiling and bouncing on her heels. She was obviously eager for me to see what was inside.

I carefully tore away the paper and opened the box. Inside was a silver charm bracelet with three charms on it. A heart. A camera. A seashell.

"The heart is for our friendship," Lily explained, peering into the box with me. "And the camera is because you're an awesome photographer and I want everyone to ask you why you have a camera on your bracelet so you can say, 'Oh, because I'm an awesome photographer.' And the shell is because of all the fun we're going to have at the beach together this summer!" She looked at me anxiously, waiting to see how I would respond.

Now it was my turn to give her a hug. "It is perfect," I said. "I love, love, love it."

She beamed.

"I especially love the heart," I croaked awkwardly, feeling my shyness creep over me. "I, well, I kind of thought you and Miranda were becoming best friends these days."

Her eyes widened. "*Miranda?* Why on earth would you think that? You're my bestie, Sara! You know that!"

I shrugged. "No reason. I guess I was just being silly."

I didn't even consider reading her thoughts.

Lily helped me clasp the bracelet around my wrist as we set off for Scoops. I loved the way it jingled and tickled my wrist ever so slightly as I walked and swung my arms. I smiled as I thought how just a little while ago I had been wishing I had an accessory to wear with my outfit, and now I had one. The most perfect one.

Lily linked arms with me as we walked to Scoops. "So Uncle Paul closed Scoops just for us tonight!" she chattered. "The trade-off is that people are welcome to buy their own ice cream, and since half the middle school is coming, he'll probably do a better business with it closed than open! Dawn Marie will be there, of course, but the rest of the staff got the night off." Dawn Marie was Lily's sort-of cousin—they weren't related by blood, but Lily called her a cousin all the same. Dawn Marie was in high school, and I know Lily looked up to her almost like a big sister.

We approached Scoops, which did look very much closed. A CLOSED sign was in the window, and no lights were on.

"I thought Miranda and Marlee and the others were here decorating," I said, puzzled.

"They are," said Lily, rapping on the door. "But Uncle Paul told us to turn off the lights while we were stringing up the decorations, so we wouldn't get a shock or whatever."

The door opened. It was Avery.

"Hey, guys," she said.

"How's the decorating going?" asked Lily as she nudged me ahead of her.

Avery stood aside to let us enter. "Great. Just great. We're—"

"SURPRISE!"

The lights flicked on. I stood there, blinking, in

total shock, as fifty or so people stood in a huge semi-circle in front of me. They were smiling. Giggling. And looking straight at me.

I still didn't get it. Confused, I looked behind me to see if Jayden was standing there.

"We so got you!" I heard Jayden's voice in front of me and turned. He stepped out of the crowd. "I cannot *believe* you thought this party was for *me*! I'm not moving for, like, two more weeks!"

Everyone laughed. When I had time to gather myself a little, I looked around. There were all my friends from school. Plus a bunch of Jayden's friends. Practically the whole boys' soccer team. The whole boys' basketball team. All of Lily's siblings. Dawn Marie. Mrs. Randazzo. Lily's aunt Angela. My dad. Lady Azura. Both of whom knew enough to hang in the back with the few other adults who were there. They knew it was a kid party. But I was really happy they were there.

I had to sit down. I staggered to a chair.

Suddenly Lily was right in front of me. "So were you truly, genuinely surprised?" she asked eagerly as she pulled up a chair and plopped down next to me.

I nodded. "Um, yes. Yes, I definitely was."

"Lady Azura was a huge help," Lily prattled on. "She and I talked about what your favorite cupcakes were, and what food we'd have, and of course your dad wanted to help too, and he suggested he take you to the aquarium today because what would I have done if you'd just shown up at my door?"

"I had no idea," I said. "I was so thrown off because I . . . I thought you and Miranda went shopping for Jayden's present yesterday!"

"We did, but we went shopping *with* him, not *for* him! He needed help picking something out for you!"

I sat back, stunned. "Oh. I thought—" I thought back on the chain of events of the past few days. Now it all made sense.

Lily's face grew serious, and she scooted her chair closer. "You of *all* people are not an easy person to surprise," she said in a low voice.

Just then Jayden loped over. "Hey," he said, grinning. "Recovered yet?"

Lily jumped up. "Got to go help Mom unload the cupcakes from the car," she said, and raced away.

Jayden occupied the chair Lily had given up. "So, were you surprised?"

"Just a little!" I said, laughing.

He laughed too, and then held out a small wrapped box. He pushed it toward me. "Here," he said. "I got you a little birthday present. No big deal or anything. Just a little something."

I was so glad I had a present for him too. "Well, I got you something too, because I was the only one who didn't get the memo that this party wasn't for you!" I said, placing my wrapped picture in front of him.

He grinned. "You first," he said.

I had to stop myself from tearing away the paper. Instead I calmly peeled away the paper to reveal a small brown box. Inside was a charm. Of a soccer ball.

"To remember me by," he said. "They had all these charms, and I wasn't sure which one you would like best, so I chose the soccer ball because that's my favorite sport. Remember the times you took pictures of me playing?"

I smiled shyly and nodded. "Thanks," I said. Little

did Jayden know, I had joined the school paper as a sports photographer just so I could take pictures of him playing! Blushing slightly, I showed him the bracelet Lily had given me.

"Yeah, I know. We all went shopping together," he said. "Good thing, too, or I would have picked you up some dumb thing, like golf clubs or something."

The charm had a little clasp on it so I was able to hook it right onto my bracelet.

"Your turn," I said after I held my wrist out so we could both admire the new charm dangling from my bracelet.

He tore off the paper and stared at the picture.

"This is awesome," he said quietly. "You did this?"

I nodded, trying to read his expression. What did he really think? What if he thought it was too personal? Too silly? Maybe his friends would tease him about it. Maybe it was not what normal girlfriends gave to normal boyfriends. . . .

"This is like, totally, completely awesome. I can't wait to show it to the guys over there. I'm going to be reading about you in the art section of the paper in a few years," he said, marveling at the picture. "You're really talented."

"Thanks," I said, feeling myself blush up to the roots of my hair.

My dad and Mrs. Randazzo carried out a big stack of pizza boxes, and everyone ate pizza for the next half hour. I moved through the throngs of people to talk with Lady Azura, who had parked herself primly in one of the booths. She sat there looking like a queen surveying her subjects, dressed up for the party in a bright-blue flowered dress with matching high-heeled shoes. Crimson lipstick and purple and blue eye shadow completed the look.

"I really appreciate your coming," I said to her.

She nodded, a little smile playing on her lips. "It has been a rather dramatic week, has it not? You have been through a lot. I am happy it was able to end this way."

"Thanks for all your help," I said, reaching down and pulling out the crystal I was still wearing around my neck. My charm bracelet tinkled pleasantly.

"You helped yourself, my dear. I simply provided some guidance along the way."

And then the lights dimmed, and Lily's mom came out, carrying a huge platter of cupcakes. One had a candle. And everyone sang "Happy Birthday" to me.

It was an amazing party. I was the happiest I'd felt in ages. Pretty much everyone I loved was in one room, gathered there for me. I couldn't remember ever feeling so special.

While people were finishing their cupcakes, laughing and talking, I looked for Lily. Something she had said to me before, about how hard it was to surprise me, was nagging at me. I wanted to see her and check in and just make sure everything was okay. I was fairly certain I was reading too much into the comment . . . but I needed to know for sure.

I found her standing near her mother, stacking dirty cups to recycle. I took her by the arm and led her to a quiet corner.

"Hey, Lil? What did you mean before? About me of all people being hard to surprise?"

She suddenly grew uncharacteristically serious, her face scrunched up in thought. "Well, you know, the biggest problem with surprise parties is that you have to be so mean to the person you're planning to surprise. You have to pretend that nobody cares about her, or remembers her birthday, or that they're all too busy to spend any time with her on her birthday. I felt so terrible pretending I didn't care that this was your birthday. It was actually Jayden's idea to pretend that the party was for him. Because I knew there was no way you wouldn't notice that I was getting ready for *some* type of party. Or someone would slip up and mention the party on Saturday in your presence. I thought that was a rather brilliant suggestion on his part."

I nodded, feeling totally relieved. *She didn't mean anything by that comment,* I thought to myself. "It was totally brilliant."

"And then," Lily continued, "there was the added challenge that it was you."

The feeling of relief froze in my chest. A shudder eddied up and down my spine. "Why did that make a difference?" I asked cautiously.

"Well, because of, you know—" Here she dropped her voice and leaned in so only I would hear. "Because of your *abilities*. I know you can do things, Sara. You don't need to keep pretending. I *am* your best friend, after all."

I looked at her, stunned. Had she just said what I thought she'd said? Did she really know about my powers?

One look at her face told me that she did.

Want to know what
happens to Sara next?

Here's a sneak peek at the next book in the series:

The Secrets
Within

I felt different today, and I didn't know why.

Was it that I was wrapped in a little girl's princess comforter and matching pink sheets? Was it the always-present warmth that filled Lily's house? For some reason, I felt younger. Watched over. Part of my best friend's family.

I liked the feeling.

I snuggled under Lily's little sister's comforter, as the morning sun poked through the eyelet-lace curtains and formed kaleidoscope patterns on the walls. Every window in the Randazzos' huge Victorian house was draped with the same curtains. Lily hated them. Too frilly. Not cool. But I liked how the curtains were all alike. They made the big house cozy.

So unlike my own house.

My house creaked with strange noises. The air hung damp and chilly, and, although Dad and Lady Azura were always there with me, it never felt cozy, because we were never alone. There were others. Some came and went, while others lingered. Not everyone could see them, but I always knew they were there.

Who were they? you might be wondering.

Ghosts.

"Do you know what I'm thinking?" Lily asked, her long, dark hair falling in a tangle around her face. Her big brown eyes glinted mischievously at me from across the room.

"No." I stifled a yawn. We'd stayed up really late talking. Mostly about Jayden, my sort of kind of first boyfriend, who had recently moved back to Atlanta. Did that make him my ex-boyfriend? I had wondered. But according to Lily, since Jayden and I were never officially going out, we never officially broke up when he moved. We just sort of said good-bye and promised to keep in touch. We'd been texting off and on, but it wasn't the same. Lily was convinced I'd meet a new boy in no time . . . she managed to change her crushes practically weekly . . . but I wasn't so sure. It had taken me twelve years to meet one Jayden. What were the odds I'd meet another one anytime soon?

I pushed myself up and faced Lily, who was stretching in her bed. Lily's four-year-old sister, Cammie, gave me her bed whenever I slept over. She always made a big drama of it, but I knew Cammie was secretly thrilled. My bed takeover was the perfect excuse to spend the night tucked between her parents.

"Come on," Lily scoffed. "You so know what I'm thinking, Sara." She raised her thick eyebrows and gave me a knowing stare.

I gulped. I'd thought we were done with that. "I don't know."

"Try harder," Lily coaxed. "Focus."

"I can't do that anymore," I protested. "The mind reading was a one-time thing. Really," I insisted. "I hate talking about this."

"Whoa!" Lily raised her arms in protest. "I was totally not going there. I was just thinking how we should challenge my lame little brothers to a pancake-eating contest. That's all."

"Oh." Color flamed my cheeks. I felt heat rise around my ears.

Lily swung her legs onto the floor. "You should trust me. I mean, I promised to never mention the mind reading, right?"

"I'm sorry," I said lamely. And I was. Truly. Lily had been my best friend ever since I'd moved to Stellamar last year. She'd stuck by me through a lot of weird stuff and never questioned me. I knew she was the real deal. Lily was loyal and never judged me. "You always keep promises," I told her. "I'm just really tired. And hungry. I bet I can down more pancakes than you."

"You're on!" Lily hurried out the door with me at her heels. And like that, my weirdness was forgotten. As always.

Recently, right before my birthday, she'd figured out I could read people's minds. She'd seen it happen, right before her eyes. I avoided talking about it, hoping and praying she hadn't put it all together . . . but she had, of course. When she finally asked me about it, I was sure she would flip out. Not want to be my friend anymore. But when I explained that the mind reading was a borrowed power—a once-in-a-lifetime, never-to-happen-again strange thing—she vowed to keep it between us. And she did. She never told Miranda or

Avery or Tamara or any of the other girls at our lunch table, girls she'd known years before I showed up. She kept my secret because we were best friends.

Sometimes I wonder if I should've trusted her with the whole truth about me.

The truth is, I can do other things. Other supernatural things. Lots of other supernatural things. I can still read minds, too, if I wanted to, but I've learned how to block that power because believe me, it's way more trouble than it's worth. The other stuff I can't block. I'm not sure anymore that I'd even want to.

I think a lot about telling her, but I'm pretty positive that even she would be weirded out by what I can do. After all, my powers weird *me* out.

"Good morning, sleepyheads!" Mr. Randazzo boomed as we entered the kitchen. He stood at the stove. His wife's frilly floral apron tied haphazardly around his waist was a stark contrast to his torn jeans and Bruce Springsteen concert T-shirt. "A tall or short stack?"

"Tall, for sure!" Lily answered for both of us. Cammie was coloring at the large oak table, and her mother, already dressed for the day in a blue shirtdress, typed on a laptop next to her. The thump of a ball hitting a baseball glove floated through the open window. "The little beasts?" Lily asked.

"Yes, your three brothers are already outside causing chaos," her dad replied as he furiously whisked pancake batter in a white ceramic bowl.

"Sam! It's getting everywhere!" Mrs. Randazzo cried.

Mr. Randazzo glanced at the batter-splattered counter and shrugged. "That's what the sponge is for. You see, girls, the secret to great pancakes is the wrist motion. Quick flicks." He demonstrated and the batter erupted, dripping over the edge of the bowl onto the already dirty counter.

Lily's mom started to stand.

"No!" her dad cried. "Lily, make her stay put. It's her day, after all."

Lily's eyes grew wide with sudden realization. She leaped forward and wrapped her mother in a massive hug. "Happy Mother's Day to you!" she sang to the tune of "Happy Birthday." Lily loved holidays. She made a big deal out of even Groundhog Day and Arbor Day. Lily sang her song all the way through, and Cammie joined in.

I stood awkwardly by the table. Mrs. Randazzo wasn't my mother. I stayed silent and watched. I'd forgotten it was Mother's Day. It wasn't a holiday I ever circled on the calendar.

Lily gently guided her mom back into her chair. "Dad has it under control."

"So he says." She glanced dubiously at the batter dotting her husband's wavy black hair, then at the dishes stacked precariously in the sink. She fingered the sticky table where earlier the boys had dripped syrup. "Maybe I'll just—"

"Just relax," Mr. Randazzo ordered. "I've got this. It's Mother's Day. Lily and Sara, entertain her. Distract her. Anything. Please."

"Are you working on the fund-raiser?" Lily slid into the chair next to her mother and purposely blocked the view of Mr. Randazzo's backhanded pancake flip.

"I'm making a chart of all the donations." Mrs. Randazzo and Lily shared the same thick dark hair, olive skin, and high cheekbones. I often thought Lily looked like a mini version of her mom. Everyone says I look like my mom too, with our blond hair and light-blue eyes. Lily's mom turned to me as if noticing I was there for the first time. "Cammie, scoot down and make room for Sara."

"I should just go." I took a tentative step backward. I didn't want to leave, but it was Mother's Day, after all. I didn't belong here. "It's a family holiday and . . ."

"Oh, get over here, silly." Mrs. Randazzo patted the place next to her. "You are so a part of this family, Sara. Believe me, I need some more girl power to balance out the boy egos in this house."

"Ego? What ego?" Mr. Randazzo called. "I am only the best pancake maker in all of the Jersey shore."

"You are needed here, Sara. Badly," Lily's mom said, smiling widely at me.

If I couldn't be with my own mom this morning, Lily's mom was definitely next best. I squeezed a chair between her and Cammie. "Hey, Camsters. I like that you're coloring the tree purple. Trees should definitely be purple."

Cammie handed me a darker shade of violet from her enormous box of crayons, and I shaded in a pine tree. Cammie's full cheeks and broad forehead resembled her dad's, but she had the same magnetic sparkle in her eyes that made everyone at school hover about Lily, like moths attracted to light.

"Ohhh, is the shoe lady coming again?" Lily asked. She raised her voice to be heard over her dad's off-key singing. *"Born to run . . . baby, we were born to run . . ."* He was forever singing Springsteen songs.

"She is." Mrs. Randazzo tapped the screen. "She promised to bring twice as many as she did last year."

"Coming where?" I asked.

"Wow, that's right, you don't know about Bargain on the Boardwalk!" Lily exclaimed.

"Bargain on the Boardwalk is a fund-raiser for the local schools that happens every year. It's next weekend, in fact," Mrs. Randazzo explained. "It's a big Stellamar tradition—kind of the unofficial kickoff to summer for the locals before the tourists descend."

"It's the most amazing flea market, but not with junky stuff," Lily added. "Well, okay, there is some junky stuff that's donated, but there's also lots of really cool crafts and accessory vendors and people selling jewelry. Last year, this lady who works for some shoe company in New York brought all these amazing shoes. You know those cute aqua sandals

I have with the chunky heels that make me almost tall? I got those for only fifteen dollars. Fifteen! Don't they look like they cost a lot more?"

"They do," I agreed, as Lily's dad set down a mountain of pancakes dripping with butter. I attempted a sincere smile as Mr. Randazzo sang, *"Hungry heart . . . ,"* but I was the only one. His Springsteen soundtrack had become background noise to his family.

"We have ten different jewelry vendors this year. This one guy, a new vendor this year, weaves together the thinnest silver wire into stunning necklaces. I know he's going to be a big hit." Mrs. Randazzo squinted at her list. "We need more stuff to be donated, though. We make the most money on the high-end rummage sale items. I do hope we get enough—"

"Don't worry about it today," Mr. Randazzo scolded. He plopped into a chair and sipped a mug of coffee, the mess by the stove and the promise of using a sponge temporarily forgotten. "Your mother needs to be stopped before she completely heads up Bargain on the Boardwalk again." She started to protest, and he gently cut her off. "It's a lot of work, honey. You can't do it all by yourself!"

"I'm going to help," Lily said, already finishing her second pancake.

"Me too," I offered. "What should I do?"

"See what you have to donate in your house. We'll take anything as long as it's clean and working," Mrs. Randazzo said.

"Sure." That sounded easy. "Hey, I bet Lady Azura has some really great stuff to donate."

"Seriously! Can you even imagine what she has? It's like opening some old-fashioned movie star's closet." Lily loved Lady Azura's style.

"Lady Azura does have classy clothes," Lily's mom said. "But for some reason, she's never given anything to the sale before."

"Really?" I was surprised. Lady Azura was quirky and more than a little odd, but she was one of the most generous people I'd ever met. Was there a reason she had never donated any of her things before?

About the Author

Phoebe Rivers had a brush with the paranormal when she was thirteen years old, and ever since then she has been fascinated by people who see spirits and can communicate with them. In addition to her intrigue with all things paranormal, Phoebe also loves cats, French cuisine, and writing stories. She has written dozens of books for children of all ages and is thrilled to now be exploring Sara's paranormal world.